MW01146510

By Mia McKenzie

These Heathens

Skye Falling

The Summer We Got Free

Black Girl Dangerous on Race, Queerness, Class and Gender

THESE HEATHENS

THESE HEATHENS

A NOVEL

MIA McKENZIE

RANDOM HOUSE NEW YORK

Random House
An imprint and division of Penguin Random House LLC
1745 Broadway, New York, NY 10019
randomhousebooks.com
penguinrandomhouse.com

LIBRARY OF CONGRESS CATALOGING-IN-PUBLICATION DATA
Names: McKenzie, Mia, author
Title: These heathens : a novel / by Mia McKenzie.
Description: First edition. | New York, NY : Random House, 2025.
Identifiers: LCCN 2025000694 |
ISBN 9780593596944 (hardcover, acid-free paper) |
ISBN 9780593596951 (ebook)
Subjects: LCGFT: Fiction | Historical fiction | Novels
Classification: LCC PS3613.C55665 T47 2025 |
DDC 813/.6—dc23/eng/20250129
LC record available at https://lccn.loc.gov/2025000694

Printed in the United States of America on acid-free paper

1st Printing

First Edition

Book design by Susan Turner

BOOK TEAM: Production editor: Ted Allen • Managing editor: Rebecca Berlant • Production manager: Samuel Wetzler • Copy editor: Madeline Hopkins • Proofreaders: Deb Bader, Amy Harned, Al Madocs

The authorized representative in the EU for product safety and compliance is Penguin Random House Ireland, Morrison Chambers, 32 Nassau Street, Dublin D02 YH68, Ireland. https://eu-contact.penguin.ie

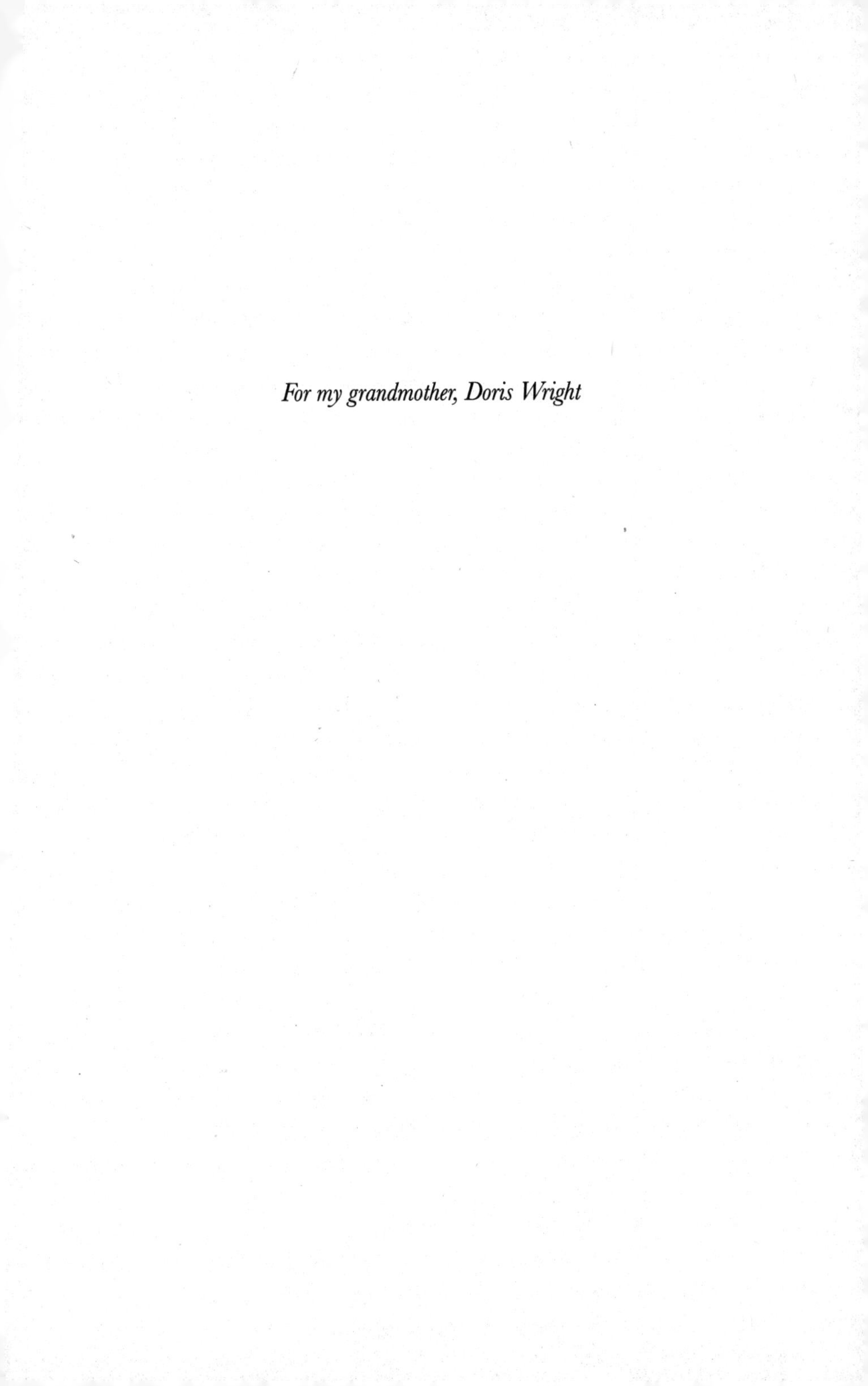

For my grandmother, Doris Wright

THESE HEATHENS

1

One thing needs clearing up right off: Reverend King was not the father. That was a rumor, started by crazy people and repeated by heathens. Reverend King had nothing to do with it. I only met the man once, and it wasn't *that kind* of meeting. Still, there's been so many insinuations, innuendos, and downright accusations over the last sixty years, I'm left with no choice but to tell the thing, the way it really happened. Which I don't appreciate. I'm old. I want to be lying in a hammock, drinking rum out a coffee mug, not setting records straight. But the Good Lord burdened me with a deep respect for the truth. So, let me say, officially: The father was nobody.

To set the story up right, I got to go back to the beginning.

I was fifteen when Ma got sick, and I had to quit school to help take care of her and Daddy and the boys. I aint want to quit, but nobody asked me what I wanted. I missed school something awful. For the first few months, I'd wonder what they were up to in math class, or what books Mrs. Lucas had assigned in English. A few times, I asked Ma and Daddy if I could go back. They both looked sorry for me, knowing how much I'd liked it, but my family needed me at home, there wasn't any way around that. Maybe once Ma got better. They said that for two years. By the time I was seventeen, I'd long since stopped thinking about school. Or maybe I just didn't have the time or energy to think about it anymore, because Ma had only gotten sicker over those years, which meant there was more to do than ever. Each morning, I got up before everyone else, to open the windows and let fresh air and light into our small house. I spent a few minutes praying and reading my Bible, then went out to feed the chickens and get eggs from the coop. I fixed breakfast for Daddy and the boys, and for myself. Ma aint really eat in the mornings anymore, but I made sure she had fresh water from the well to drink, and I laid out clean clothes for her just in case she wanted to get dressed. I got the boys dressed, and their faces washed as well as I could with them squirming around the whole time. I packed beans and bread, or cold chicken, for Daddy's lunch, and after he left for work, I walked the boys the first quarter mile to school, then let them go on the rest of the way with their friends. When I got back home, I checked in on Ma before cleaning up from breakfast. Then I went out back to start the washing. That was all before eight o'clock, and there was plenty more after that, but I reckon you got the gist. Point is, there wasn't time left in a day for thinking about things I couldn't have—school or otherwise. I aint have a choice but to do it all, so I did, and I didn't resent it. Jesus watched over me, kept me safe and loved, and I was grateful. I'd be lying if I said I *liked* my life, but no colored girl in rural Georgia could say that in 1960. She either had it real bad or she had it okay, and I had it okay, right on. So, I thanked God every chance I got and didn't waste time dreaming.

"Close the shades, please," Ma told me one morning when I'd gone in her room to see if she needed anything before I cleaned up from breakfast. "It too bright out today."

It was the middle of October, and the day was cloudy as a cataract, but I went ahead and started closing all the shades, anyhow.

"What wrong with you?"

I turned around and looked at her, confused. "Ma?"

She was raised up on her elbow, peering at me. "It something different about you, child."

I shook my head. Every day was the same, and I was the same every day. I couldn't remember the last time something was different about me.

She stared at me a moment longer, then seemed to run out of interest, or energy, I couldn't tell which. She lay back on the bed and was asleep again before I got out the room.

One thing I liked about my life was the moments I had to myself, especially the few minutes between starting the laundry and when Ma came out to sit with me while I did it. No matter how sick or tired she felt in the morning, she always ended up coming out to sit with me on the back porch while I washed clothes. But for the first little while, fifteen minutes or so, I was out there by myself. These were my favorite minutes. We had a record player that Daddy had found broken somewhere and fixed, and sometimes I'd put on Mahalia Jackson while I worked, but not for that first little bit. I let it be quiet. There was always noise—the neighbors' dogs barking, somebody's baby screaming, everybody's chickens bawking—but I could block it out, make a quiet space inside my head while I mixed up the soap and water. On the morning Ma said there was something different about me, I filled the quiet space with thoughts about last Sunday's church service while I poured the washing powder into the bucket. Pastor Mills had let his daughter, Constance, lead a hymn, even though the girl couldn't sing. Deacon Turner, who always sucked up to Pastor, had the nerve to say the girl sang "like a bird ascending toward heaven." I was scandalized to see somebody lie so bad in church. I knew Jesus could hear us no matter where we were, but you couldn't get a word past him in his own house. "A bird ascending toward heaven"? More like a bird getting shot out a tree. That thought made me laugh. I took out the little notebook I kept in my pocket, and the pencil I kept in my hair, and wrote it down. I'd been doing that—writing down little funny thoughts and turns of phrase—for as long as I could remember. I used to use little scraps of paper I'd tear from the corner of *The Millen News,* or a paper grocery bag, or whatever was handy at the moment I had the thought. But most times I'd end up losing the scrap of paper, and the thought right along with it. When I quit school, Mrs. Lucas, who'd seen me writing thoughts on scraps of paper for a whole year, gave me a little notebook as a present. I liked it much better than the scraps, so once I'd filled it up, I went out and got another one. I'd filled up half a dozen little notebooks by now. I kept them in my bottom dresser drawer, and sometimes I'd take them out and look over what I'd written, when I had time, which I almost never did.

"Doris Steele!" It was Mrs. Haley, our neighborhood's official crazy person, coming up behind the house.

"Ma'am?" I called out to her, hoping I wouldn't have to come down off the porch. But she leaned against the wood fence and waved me over to her. Crazy as she was, she was still my elder, so I had to be polite. I went down the steps and crossed the yard. Soon as I was within reach, she put a gnarled hand on my stomach and, with raised, crooked, penciled-on eyebrows, said, "I can feel life pulsing inside your belly, Doris Steele."

I shook my head and took a step back. "I'm pretty sure that's just Cream of Wheat, ma'am."

She threw her head back and cackled at the cataract sky.

Mrs. Haley was sho'nuff crazy, and it didn't make sense to take anything she said to heart. But right then it hit me that my menses was late. So late, in fact, that I couldn't remember when it came last. On top of that, I'd been queasy on and off the last few days. Standing there, watching Mrs. Haley, who was laughing herself to tears now, I remembered what Ma had said. "It something different about you, child."

Shit.

I left Mrs. Haley standing there and ran in the house.

I went to my room and got down on my knees beside the bed. My first prayer was: *Lord Jesus, please don't let me be pregnant.* But even as I said it, I already knew I was. So, next I prayed: *Please take it away, Lord.* But that didn't sound right, either. If I was pregnant, then it must be God's will. What sense did it make to pray to that same God to take it away?

I got up off my knees and sat down on the bed. I thought about God's will. I thought about my own. And I decided.

I have to get rid of it.

I was sure of that, though I didn't know why I was so sure. Truth is, my certainty surprised me, because I feared God and all the ways he might punish me for even thinking such a sinful thing. But deep in my soul, I knew I had to do it.

I hadn't been back inside Burgess Landrum since I left it two years before, but it hadn't changed. I went straight to Room 107, stood outside the classroom door, and peeked in through the glass pane. I knew most of the students, since almost all of them lived in Millen. Ours was a town of only about thirty-five hundred people. I'd gone to school with these kids all my life. From the doorway, I could see my cousin Ernestine sitting in the front row, and my best friend, Lena, staring all dreamy out the window. Marvin, who we called *Perv*in, because he was always trying to look up some girl's skirt, sat in the back with his legs stretched out into the aisle, like he owned the place.

And there at the front was Mrs. Lucas. "'There is always something left to love,'" she was saying, quoting *A Raisin in the Sun* without looking down at the book, her eyes scanning the room from where she stood leaning against her desk. "What does Mama mean when she says this to Beneatha?"

"Do it mean loving bad people?" asked Lena, who'd tuned in at the mention of love.

Mrs. Lucas tilted her head to one side in that way she sometimes did when asking a question. "Is Walter Lee a bad person?"

"Naw, he just stupid," said Marvin, and some of the others

laughed. Shamed as I am to admit it, if I was having a bad day and running low on compassion, I sometimes thought of Marvin and that whole bunch as "the Dumbasses," because nary a one of them could've poured piss out a boot, even if the instructions were written on the heel. But Mrs. Lucas never seemed to mind Marvin's foolishness. She gave him a smile that was kind and firm, both, and he settled right on down.

"He aint stupid, but he make bad choices," Ernestine corrected Marvin. Then, looking at Mrs. Lucas, she said, "So, it mean loving people even when they make bad choices."

"Bad choices," Mrs. Lucas agreed, nodding, "or mistakes. Or don't live up to our hopes or expectations. Because that's when we need love the most. Isn't it?"

When she said those words, I knew I'd made the right decision going down there. Of course it should be her I told, if I was going to tell anybody, and I *had* to tell somebody. It couldn't be Daddy or Ma. It couldn't be Lena, who, much as I loved her, couldn't keep a confidence if our Lord and Savior Jesus Christ came down from heaven and pinky swore her to secrecy himself. Mrs. Lucas was my favorite teacher. And I liked to think I was her favorite student. She always used to say to me, "Doris, you sure do know how to turn a phrase." That made me feel good because Mrs. Lucas was from Atlanta, and she'd studied English at Spelman. She knew words better than anybody. I liked her because of that, and because she was clever, and quiet right up until the moment loudness was called for—like when she needed to snap one of the Dumbasses in line—and sometimes she got swept away by her own emotions. I'd seen her get teary in class, always over some pretty passage in a book. I'd cried right along with her, even when I wasn't all that moved by the words, because I was moved by the fact that she was moved. I was moved by her. One time sophomore year, while Marvin was giving a book report so middling that a dog could've thought it up while sniffing another dog's ass, Mrs. Lucas had burst into tears. In Marvin's defense, her husband had recently been killed in a car crash, so it wasn't all on account of his shitty schoolwork. Later that same day, she'd gone to Mr. Hammond and persuaded him to give me extra time to finish my math assignments, since Ma was sick and all. Mrs. Lucas was always like that, always helpful, always looking out for me, even in her own times of trial and tribulation. All the time I'd known her, she'd never once let me down.

A few minutes later, class ended, and I waited at the door while everybody hurried out. When Lena saw me, she said, "Doris! What you doing here?"

"I come to say hey to Mrs. Lucas," I told her.

"What for?"

I shrugged. "I just felt like it. The Lord put it on my heart, I guess."

She gave me a look like she thought that was a strange thing for the Lord to put on my heart, but she left it alone.

"You want to come over and watch *As the World Turns*?" she asked me.

"Girl, you know I can't," I said.

"Well, I'll walk back home with you."

"I don't know how long I'll be talking to Mrs. Lucas."

"I thought you was just saying hey."

"Sure," I said, "but I aint seen her in a while. We got a lot to catch up on."

"Alright, I'll wait," Lena said.

"Don't wait. I'll catch up with you."

Lena frowned and I could tell she wanted to argue, but she didn't. I used to go to Lena's after school, to watch television and do homework, when Ma was healthy. She knew I'd been through a lot the last couple of years, so she never gave me a hard time about anything anymore. Still, I knew she missed the old days. I missed them, too. She slung her bag over her shoulder, shrugged, and said, "Alright, then, I'll walk slow."

Once Lena was gone, I had to wait for Marvin—who always moved like he had nowhere to be and nobody to see when he got there—to leave. He took a short eternity packing up his books and I would've thought he was going slow on purpose so he could watch Mrs. Lucas erase the blackboard, the way he always used to with our history teacher. But, Mrs. Lucas wasn't Miss Bradley. Miss Bradley had a backside so perfectly curved, looked like it was formed by the hand of God himself, on a Sunday, when he should've been napping but couldn't help but get up and make one more perfect thing. Mrs. Lucas didn't have that kind of backside. She wasn't *sexy*. She was attractive—she had smooth skin, long eyelashes, and a pretty smile; she wore a modest amount of makeup; she had a smallish bosom and a slim figure, which she kept covered up in one or another respectable swing dress—but I didn't think she was striking in any way that might cause ogling.

When Marvin finally shuffled out the room, I stepped

toward Mrs. Lucas. I stood watching her, noticing the way some hairs that had come loose from the neat bun she always wore shook gently against her collar with each wide sweep of the eraser. I felt my mouth get dry at the thought of what I was about to say. I watched while she erased the board, feeling the dryness in my mouth move to my throat, and when she finally put down the eraser and turned around and saw me standing there, I said, "I'm pregnant." And just like that it was out, like a cat set loose.

Mrs. Lucas bit her lip for what felt like a long time, a full minute at least. But it probably wasn't any more than the time one long, deep breath takes to get in and out of the lungs. She didn't say anything at first, just stood there, silent. I thought I saw a slight shake of her head, and a hint of a heartbroken look in her eyes. Then, "Doris," she began. It sounded like a question, so I reckoned she was going to get right to it and ask who the father was. But then she didn't finish the sentence. Or maybe my name was all she meant to say in the first place, a sad reminder to herself of who she'd thought I was before that moment. I couldn't bear to have her think she wasted two years believing I was special, and now I'd turned out to be just a common girl, sweet-talked by some common boy, and knocked up.

I understand now that's not what was on her mind at all. That the slight shake of her head, the hint of a heartbroken look in her eyes, was just worry. But I'd been raised on shame, gorged and fattened on it, like all the girls around me, so I panicked.

"I filled up the notebook you give to me when I left school," I told her. "And plenty more since. Sometime, I wake up in the middle of the night to write down something I thought up in a dream."

She looked like she wasn't sure what I was getting at. But she reached out and took my hand, anyhow. "Oh, Doris," she said. "I know you must be scared right now—"

"I need to not be pregnant no more," I said, pushing full steam ahead with the damn thing. Ashamed or not, I knew I didn't want a baby.

Mrs. Lucas opened her mouth to speak, but nothing came out, so she closed it and bit her lip again. I'd never seen her without words before. *Good job, Doris,* I told myself. *You broke Mrs. Lucas's perfect brain. You sure as shit going to hell for this, let alone baby-murder.*

Baby-murder. That's how I thought of it. That's what Pastor Mills had called it, just two Sundays ago, in a sermon about the breakdown of the family, and I'd believed every word. I still believed it. And I knew it was possible, even more like than not, that Mrs. Lucas, who I thought of as a good, God-fearing Christian woman, felt the same way about it as Pastor Mills, and that she'd see me as a heathen for even bringing it up. But none of that stopped me from wanting it gone.

"Will you help me?" I was surprised when I heard the tremor in my own voice. I didn't mean to sound desperate, but I reckon I was. Then, all of a sudden, I was sobbing.

Mrs. Lucas put her hand on my arm. "Of course I'll help you."

Years later, when we went back over it all, she told me that in that moment she was thinking about herself at seventeen, also pregnant, on her knees every night praying for a miscarriage, which eventually, mercifully, came. At the time, she'd thanked God for it. But, when she looked back on it? It was simple good luck she felt grateful to. And now, here was her favorite student, seventeen and pregnant and looking for some good luck herself. "Of course I will," she said again, and for a moment it was the way it had always been when I came to her with a question about a book or some deeper meaning in a poem, or in my life, and she'd say, *Sit down, sugar. Let's think this through.* But then she hesitated. "Doris," she asked, "do Babe and J.D. know?"

"No, ma'am."

She waited a moment, maybe thinking I was going to say more. When I didn't, she went on. "Doris, I want to help you. But it doesn't seem right for me to go behind your parents' backs and—"

"*They* backs aint got no more to do with it than Harry Belafonte's. *They* not the ones pregnant. If you tell them, they'll say it's God's will, that even to think about getting rid of it is a one-way ticket to perdition. And twenty or thirty Bible verses later, I'll still be pregnant with a baby I'm *dead set* on not having."

"Are you sure you're pregnant?" she asked me.

I nodded. I was sure.

Mrs. Lucas was staring at my belly, her brown eyes heavier than I'd ever seen them, except in the months after her husband died. She was thinking about that husband then, wondering what he'd say if he knew what she was thinking about doing. Probably something like, *Woman, have you lost your mind?* And then try to talk her out of it. But he was dead, so his opinion mattered less to her than it might otherwise. And, anyhow, in the years since his death, she'd had a whole bunch of thoughts he wouldn't like if he knew about them. So, she moved to the door, opened it and peeked out to make sure nobody was there, then shut it again. She pulled my chair up next to hers and made for me to sit, and I did. Then she sat down, clasped her hands in her lap, and said, "Alright, Doris. How can I help you, sugar?"

"I need somebody to do it," I told her. "But I don't know nobody I can ask." I knew about two granny midwives who, along with birthing babies, were said to also "bring back menses" from time to time. But both of them knew my folks—one even went to our church—and I couldn't risk Ma and Daddy finding out what I was up to and putting a stop to it.

"Do you have money for an abortion?" Mrs. Lucas asked.

It was the first time either of us had said the word. It sounded so strange to my ears. *Abortion.* It almost rhymed with *misfortune*, but not quite.

"I got fifteen dollars I saved from picking peanuts," I told her. "How much do it cost?"

"Depends who does it. A doctor's gonna cost more than fifteen dollars," she said. "A granny midwife might cost more or less."

"You know somebody who can do it?"

She named the two women I already knew of.

"I can't ask neither one of them. They might tell my folks."

"They wouldn't," Mrs. Lucas said. "Keeping secrets is part of their job."

I studied on her point, then pushed the thought away. I couldn't risk it. "Don't you know nobody else?"

"Lots of people can do it," she said. "But I don't know, offhand, anyone else I'd feel safe taking you to. Women die from bad abortions, Doris."

"Yes, ma'am."

I'd known a woman who died from one, a neighbor who used to watch me sometimes when I was small, a mean woman I'd never liked called Miss Janice. After she died, my folks and their friends had talked freely about the cause. I was seven then and it was the first time I'd ever heard of such a thing as an abortion. That night, I'd had a dream about Miss Janice. She told me she aint regret it. "I'd rather had died than have another kid I didn't want sucking the life out of me." Which I thought was an evil thing to say with her other children sitting right there, dream or not.

"I might know someone who knows someone," Mrs. Lucas said, more talking to herself than to me. "But it's complicated."

"Complicated how?" I asked.

She didn't answer.

"Ma'am," I said, "I don't want to be pushy. I sho don't. But I aint getting no less pregnant. Tell the truth, I'm more pregnant now than I was just a few days ago."

She laughed. I almost reached for my notebook, to write that down, but I reckoned I ought to wait.

Mrs. Lucas nodded and said, "Alright. I'll call her."

I could've shit, I was so relieved.

"But, Doris," Mrs. Lucas said, "you can't tell anyone about this. I'm not your teacher anymore but my involvement would be frowned upon."

To put it mild, I thought. "I won't ever tell nobody."

"Good." Then she asked: "Are you sure an abortion is what you want?"

"I can't support a baby," I told her. "And I don't think I'm old enough to be a good mother."

"Women your age have babies every day," she said.

I fixed my mouth to tell her I was not a woman. It was a strange thing to almost say, because until that moment I was sure I was one. *A grown-ass woman and don't you forget it.* But right then? Faced with motherhood? I felt like a terrified girl-child in need of a mother herself.

"You could have it and give it up," she said.

I shook my head. "My folks aint gon' let me do that."

She nodded. "Alright," she said. "Is there anybody lives near you who has a telephone?"

"No, ma'am."

"Well, then, come back here again tomorrow, after school. I should know by then whether or not my friend can help."

"Yes, ma'am."

She reached out and took my hand, held it, squeezed. "Everything's going to be alright, Doris."

I thought about the squishy something clinging to my womb. "What if it aint?"

Mrs. Lucas took my other hand and squeezed that one, too. "It will be," she said.

And because she'd never lied to me before, I believed her.

2

Lena wasn't lying when she said she'd walk slow. I caught up to her about a quarter mile from the school, and we walked the rest of the way home together. There was no school bus service for black students in Jenkins County at the time, so you had to walk the two miles each way, rain or shine. Lena was preoccupied with boys, as usual. On this day, it was two senior-class boys, Tony and Allen, who were walking way up ahead of us.

"Who you think more fine?" she asked me, nodding toward the boys' lanky frames. It wasn't the first time she asked me that question. Before I quit school, it was a regular point of discussion on our walks home.

Neither of the boys was all that fine to me. Tony, who was high-yellow with freckles, reminded me of a ventriloquist's dummy I'd seen on TV. Every time he spoke to me, I thought about a white man's hand up the back of his overalls, and it just wasn't sexy. Allen, on the other hand, was basic brown and freckle-free. His face didn't call to mind ventriloquists' dummies, or puppets generally, but he had a backside that stood out like a shelf, and every time I saw him I got distracted wishing I had a cold drink to set down on it.

Now, don't misunderstand me. I liked boys, and they liked me back. I was a pretty girl—dimple cheeked and buxom—and boys had been sniffing around me long as I could remember. I'd kissed a bunch, let a few slide a hand up my blouse, and went further with a couple of them, all along praying to Jesus to deliver me from my sinful desires. I was pretty sure I'd want to marry a man, one day. So, yes. I liked them alright. I just didn't see what all the *fuss* was about. I didn't see why girls got stupid over boys. I knew girls who got in fistfights with other girls over boys. I'd once watched a grown woman cry and beg a man not to leave her, right in the road where everyone could see. Mascara running down her face, knees getting scraped on the hard, dry dirt, the whole shebang! And it just plain didn't make sense to me. Far as I could tell, only half of boys and men were kind on their best day, and that's if I'm being generous. Daddy was a kind man. But I could easily name an evil Negro for every one of him. Of the kind ones, maybe a quarter were also nice to look at. Don't even bother throwing in brains, or a love of words, 'cause you'd be down to one in twenty by then. Even if you had better-than-middling luck, the best you could expect to get was a good, dumb one. Or you might land a handsome but evil somebody. Or a smart one with a face like a possum's ass. Or, worse, a face like a possum's face. And, depending on what any particular woman liked, any of those options might be fine. But none of them would be something to get your ass beat or let your mascara run in the street over. Looking at Tony and Allen walking in the hot sun, it seemed reasonable to me to love a man and let him leave, if leaving was what he was set on doing. Forget him like a song from last summer.

"Allen, I reckon," I told Lena, reaching in my pocket for my little notebook. It wasn't there, but I found a receipt from the grocer. I took the pencil from behind my ear and scrawled: *Forget him like a song from last summer.*

"Allen" was the same answer I always gave, but Lena still nodded, excited, like we were discussing it for the first time. "Yeah, I think so, too!"

We got to Lena's house first, and we said goodbye, and I walked the rest of the way home. I stopped in the outhouse, then found my younger brothers playing marbles on the front porch. They walked back together from the elementary school. I asked if they brought any schoolwork home.

"Just some reading," said Jack, who was nine.

I told him to go inside and get reading, then. He said, "Woman, can't you see we playing marbles?"

Bud, who was seven, giggled.

"If y'all don't get in the house," I said, "you gon' lose some real marbles."

Jack gave me a look like he didn't believe a word of that, since I'd never made good on a threat to go upside either of their heads before. But they went on inside anyway, as a courtesy.

I was just about to follow when I felt such a strong wave of nausea that I almost gave up my lunch right there on the porch planks. Only by the grace of God did I make it back to the outhouse.

When I was done, I washed my face in the bucket of water I'd pulled from the well that morning, then I went on inside and knocked on Ma's door. I heard her say, "Come in," so I did. The room was dark, and she was lying in bed, on her side, curled up like a baby in the womb. "Ma? You need anything?"

"Naw," she said. "Just to rest a bit longer."

I shut the door, quiet.

When I came back out into the front room, Jack looked worried. "You sick, Doris? You throwed up?"

"I must'a ate something bad. Where Bud?" I asked, looking around.

Jack shrugged.

I found Bud in the kitchen, eating jam with a spoon, straight out the jar. I almost felt sick again. I thought about making another threat against his marbles but my heart wasn't in it. Instead, I took the jar, gave him a bucket, and told him to go fill it up at the well so I could fix supper.

I didn't think about the pregnancy. When it bubbled up in my mind, I pushed it back.

By the time our father got home, Jack had finished his reading and the boys were back on the porch. I heard Daddy greet them cheerfully, even though his voice sounded tired. Then he came on in the kitchen, looking worn out in dirty overalls, his face smudged with some kind of car grease, but smiling, saying, "Smell good in here, Doris. You cooking like your ma more and more."

I spent the next day half-asleep, moving through my chores

in a daze. By the time I got to the high school and sat down at one of the desks in Mrs. Lucas's classroom, I could've just as easily crawled up under it and slept there until morning.

"How you feeling today, Doris?" Mrs. Lucas asked me.

I was feeling like warmed-over shit. But I said, "Just tired, ma'am," because I was taught not to complain, lest the Lord find me ungrateful for all he'd given to me and take it all away in a fit of wrath. Which, now that I thought about it, did make Almighty God sound fickle.

"Well, I'll get right to it, then," Mrs. Lucas said. "I found someone who can help you. An old friend of mine knows a doctor."

"A doctor?" I asked. I'd been hoping for a granny midwife. Doctors scared me a little. But then again, I knew I had no business being choosy.

"A *colored* doctor," she said. "He studied medicine in France, and he's licensed there."

"What he doing here?"

"He was born and raised in Atlanta. He's back in Georgia, just for the year, seeing to some family business."

I considered all this. A colored doctor seemed the next best thing to a granny midwife. "How much it gon' cost?"

"Nothing," she said. "Sylvia's offered to pay for it."

"Sylvia?"

"Mrs. Broussard. The old friend I mentioned. We grew up together in Atlanta. I told her about you and she offered to pay for the whole thing."

I stared at her, stunned. "How come?"

Mrs. Lucas thought about it awhile. Then she said, "Because she has a lot of money and she likes finding new ways to spend it. Funding some poor girl's abortion is probably more exciting for her than buying another television set."

I'd known Mrs. Lucas was from Atlanta, and I'd always heard folks say she came from money. So, it didn't shock me that she had a friend there who could afford to pay for my abortion like it was nothing. Still, I didn't know what to think. It felt wrong to let a stranger foot the bill for such a sinful thing. If I was going to have an abortion, it ought to cost me something. How else would the Lord know how bad I felt about it? On the other hand, who was I to say no to the most generous offer anybody had ever made me?

"When would it get done?"

"Tomorrow afternoon," she said. "But Sylvia wants us to come early."

"Come where?"

"To her home, in Collier Heights. She wants to meet you. She says she wouldn't feel comfortable doing this kind of thing for a girl she's never met. But I think she probably just wants some company."

"She lonely?"

"She might be."

Collier Heights was a suburb of Atlanta. Lena had a well-off auntie who lived there, and she told me it was a neighborhood full of colored people with money. She said they sometimes had "dinner parties" where they moved from house to house, starting with appetizers in one house, moving to somebody else's house for a main course, eventually ending up at a whole different house for dessert. I couldn't see any sane person being lonely in a place like that. I imagined Mrs. Lucas's friend as a crotchety, rich biddy, the type of woman who wore black in mourning of a husband who'd been dead so long she had to look at his picture to remember his face, and who sat judging her neighbors with narrowed eyes through lace curtains. I didn't know any women like that, mind you. I must've seen the image in a movie or read about it in a book. I didn't relish the thought of spending time with such a person. Then again, a woman like that didn't seem like to approve of what I was doing, let alone pay for it. So, maybe she wasn't some old biddy after all. Either way, meeting her seemed like a small price to pay.

"Alright, then. When do we go?"

"Now."

"Now?"

"Well, soon. Sylvia's invited us for dinner."

"I can't go *now*. I got to get home and look after my brothers. I got to make supper." What was she thinking? I couldn't just run off to Atlanta on a moment's notice. "Can't we go in the morning?"

"Will it be any easier to get away in the morning?" she asked.

It wouldn't be. On Saturdays, I had to watch the boys while fixing breakfast, same as every day. Then I had to do the wash, same as every day.

"How long we'll be gone?" I asked.

"We'll come back Sunday."

I just stared at her, mouth flopped open like an old pocketbook. What could I even say?

"I know it's a lot on short notice, Doris. And I told Sylvia you might not be able to do it. But this is the best chance we have of solving your problem without creating any new ones. Sylvia will set the whole thing up and let you rest at her house after. That way if, God forbid, anything goes wrong, the doctor will be close by. Besides, no one knows you in Atlanta, do they?"

I shook my head, no. Atlanta wasn't but three hours away by train, but I'd never been there.

"Then there's no chance of anything getting back to your folks," Mrs. Lucas said.

She had a point.

"My family gon' be worried sick if I just disappear," I told her.

"Don't just disappear," she said. "Leave a note."

"Saying what?"

"You're a smart girl, Doris," she said. "I know you can figure it out."

She drove me home. When we pulled up outside my house, she said, "Meet me back at the school in an hour and a half. We'll drive to the Augusta train station. We're less likely to be seen by anyone who knows you over there. We'll take the train from there to Atlanta. Don't drink anything. It's a long trip and there are no colored restrooms along the way."

My brothers were out on the porch playing marbles again. Jack looked up at me, expecting me to scold them, but I went on past them into the house. Ma was in her room resting, as usual for this time of day. There was a pot of black-eyed peas simmering low on the burner. I knew this meant Ma wanted Hoppin' John for supper, and for me to make the rice to go with it, and I was glad of that because rice cooked fast. I got right to it, filling a pot with water, setting it to boil while I washed and sorted the grains and then dumped them into the water.

I went into the room I shared with my brothers, opened a dresser drawer, and stared into it. I wasn't sure what I should pack. Plenty of underwear, I reckoned. A sweater, in case the nights got cool in Atlanta this time of the year, same as here. But then I remembered folks saying it was always warmer in the city than out in the sticks. So maybe I wouldn't need a sweater after all.

I didn't have a suitcase, on account of never having been anywhere, but Daddy had an old one in the kitchen closet, shoved behind the mop and broom. Soon as I walked back into the kitchen, Bud came in. "Whatchu doin', Doris?"

"Nothing," I told him. "Go play."

"I aint 'pose to be playing. I'm 'pose to be reading. Aint you gon' fuss at me 'bout it?"

"Not right now," I said.

He stared at me another moment, then whispered, "I need a little jam."

"What for?" I asked him.

"Whatchu mean, *what for*? To *eat*. What else?"

I frowned at him, then opened the kitchen closet, pushed the mop and broom aside, and got out the suitcase. But then I thought about walking to the school with it, and how I might call attention to myself. So, I put it back. I returned to my room. Bud followed, and watched me as I pulled the pillowcase off my pillow and started putting clothes in it.

"What you doing that for?"

"Nothing."

"Must be for *something,*" he said.

I ignored him and went back out into the kitchen, where the rice was boiling. I lowered the fire and, after waiting a minute, put a top on the pot. I wanted to check in on Ma before I left, but I was worried she'd ask me to do something—like make cornbread to go with supper—that would keep me from meeting Mrs. Lucas.

When I went back into our room, Bud was sitting on my bed beside the stuffed pillowcase, plundering through it with his grubby little hands.

"Get on out of there!" I told him, pushing his hands away.

"What you need so many underwears for?"

"None of your business, that's what. Go on back outside, now."

He frowned and I knew I'd hurt his feelings. He was sensitive.

"Listen here," I said. "I got to go somewhere. But I be back. I need you and Jack to look after Ma until Daddy get home. Can you do that?"

He made a face like he wasn't sure, like he was scared.

I put my hand on his shoulder. "It's okay. She probably gon' stay sleep. If she wake up, she might call for a glass of water or something. That's all. You can do that, can't you? You tall enough to reach in the cupboard if you stand on the stool, aint you?"

He nodded. "I'm tall enough," he said, looking proud.

I felt a surge of love for him, sweet little ole jam-eating somebody that he was.

When I was done packing a couple of days' worth of clothes, some toiletries, and my Bible, I sent Bud back out to the front porch, to play marbles with Jack and one of his friends from down the road who'd joined him. I checked the pots of peas and rice to make sure they were both done and then turned them off.

I found a piece of paper and a pencil and wrote a note. It said: *Dearest Ma and Daddy, Don't worry about me. Our Lord and Savior Jesus Christ is watching over me. I'll be back Sunday. Love, Doris.* I put the note on the table. I picked up the pillowcase and opened the back door, just as Lena was coming up the back steps. "What you doing here?" I asked her.

"You been acting funny," she said.

"Naw, I aint."

"I known you every day of our lives, aint I? I ought to know if you acting funny or not. And you sho is. So, come on and tell me why."

"It aint nothing to tell, Lena."

"You lying," she said. "I know 'cause your eyebrow twitching."

"I *aint* lying."

"Swear it on Jesus. Swear it on Jesus it aint nothing funny going on with you."

"I aint swearing it on Jesus or nothing else," I told her. "You just gon' have to believe me."

She pointed at the pillowcase I'd forgotten I was holding. "What you got in there?"

Damn it. I didn't have time for this.

I took Lena's arm and steered her away from the door, pulling it closed behind me, and down the back steps. "Listen," I told her. "I'm gon' tell you something, but you can't tell nobody. *Nobody.* You understand?"

"Sho," she said.

"Swear it. On Jesus."

"I swear it on Jesus. I can keep a secret, Doris."

She couldn't keep a secret. I knew that. But I had to go, and I couldn't think what else to do but tell her, get the hell out of there, and worry about it later, after the thing was done. "I'm pregnant."

Her eyes got wide. "Ooooh!"

I took her arm and pulled her farther away from the house. I put the pillowcase down on the ground.

"I'm gon' get rid of it."

She covered her mouth with her hand, looking scandalized. But she didn't say anything.

"You can't tell nobody, Lena," I said again. "You swore."

She just stared at me. I shook her arm. "You hear me?"

She nodded.

"I got to go. I be back Sunday," I told her, picking up the pillowcase. I left her standing there and headed for the school.

• • •

Mrs. Lucas was waiting in her car outside Burgess Landrum. I double-checked no one was around and then slipped into the back, lying down on the seat the way she'd told me to do until we got to the train station in Augusta.

"Alright?" she asked, without turning around.

"Yes, ma'am."

Without another word, she pulled out the lot and onto the street.

3

Both my folks were born in rural Georgia, dirt poor from day one, without a pot to piss in or a window to throw it out of. By the time me and my brothers came along, they were better off, but not by a lot. We never had much money, and after Ma got sick we had even less. I knew that Negroes who had money existed. The Sammy Davises and Josephine Bakers of the world, and the colored doctors and business owners I read about in *Jet* magazine. But I'd never been closely acquainted with a wealthy Negro myself. Which is why the first thing I noticed, when I saw Mrs. Sylvia Broussard that day, was the quality of her clothing. She was wearing plaid pedal pushers, a starched white classic button-down blouse, and kitten heel slingbacks, and every single thread looked expensive, like the clothes I'd seen on display in shop windows in downtown Augusta. The next thing I noticed was the car parked in her driveway, a very new-looking Studebaker Lark convertible that was so shiny I could see a pimple on my forehead reflected in its chrome. Then there was the house—brick, one story, sprawling, surrounded by trees, and easily five times the size of any house I'd ever been inside of. Our house in Millen wasn't a whole lot bigger than Mrs. Broussard's front porch, from which she waved to us when we pulled up in the car she'd sent, along with a gray-haired driver, to pick us up at the train station. She was light-skinned, wavy-haired, and thin as a switch. And, I realized, I recognized her. Two years before, I'd seen her sitting with Mrs. Lucas's family at Mr. Lucas's funeral. I'd noticed her then because she was wearing a fur stole so luxurious, looked like the mink wasn't all the way dead yet. Now, she stood on her driveway, her arms held out to Mrs. Lucas, her eyes bright with affection and at the same time heavy with the threat of tears, as she said, "Catie. You came. I wasn't sure you actually would."

Mrs. Lucas looked embarrassed by the greeting. Her smooth brown cheeks got reddish, and she laughed, nervous, then said, "Of course we came. We're grateful for your help, Syl," and hugged her. When they parted, Mrs. Lucas nodded toward me. "This is Doris."

"Well, it must be," said Mrs. Broussard.

"Afternoon, ma'am."

"Afternoon," she replied, sort of looking me over. "She's pretty for a dark-skinned girl, isn't she?" she said to Mrs. Lucas. Then, to me: "Between those cheekbones and that bosom, it's no surprise you're in the family way. You must have boys waiting in line to knock you up."

This should have been my first clue that Mrs. Broussard was a heathen. No God-fearing woman I knew, especially one with home training, would talk so casually about sex, and to a girl she just met five seconds ago. But I chalked it up to nerves. She *seemed* nervous, sho'nuff, almost awkward, as she stood

there putting her hands in her pockets and taking them out again, cracking her knuckles with her thumbs. And considering the favor she was doing for me, it seemed only right that I should give her the benefit of the doubt.

"Sylvia," Mrs. Lucas said, in a tone that was a whole lecture by itself.

"What?" Mrs. Broussard asked. "It's a compliment." She reached out and put her hand on my arm. "You take it as a compliment, Doris."

"Yes, ma'am," I said.

She smiled approvingly at me, and then made a sweeping gesture toward the house. "Well, y'all come on inside and get the tour."

Mrs. Broussard's house turned out to be even bigger on the inside than it looked from the driveway. We passed under the haint blue ceiling of the porch and entered into a hallway that extended all the way to the back of the house, with rooms off either side of it. All along the walls of this hallway, there were framed artworks and sculptures, of different styles and time periods and subject matters, but all depicting colored folks. There was a painting of a jazz band playing on a street corner, the colors so loud and happy you could almost hear the horns, and another of a woman in a wide-brimmed hat, lying under a tree, sunlight peeking at her through the leaves. Just inside the front door there was a painting of Mrs. Broussard holding hands with a man I reckoned was her husband, while three young children sat smiling at their feet. A painting on the op-

posite wall showed two women reading together on an expensive-looking sofa in an expensive-looking room. One of the women looked like Mrs. Broussard and the other one looked a whole lot like Mrs. Lucas. I wondered if it was her, but I felt too shy to ask. And that wasn't the only thing I felt too shy to ask about.

Because there were no colored restrooms along the train route, I needed to pee something awful. But I was embarrassed to say so. Maybe rich Negroes thought it was uncouth to talk about going to the toilet. Standing in that hallway, looking at all that fancy art and expensive furniture, I just couldn't bring myself to ask for the head. But I didn't have to. "There's a restroom right here," was the first thing Mrs. Broussard said when we got inside, pointing to a door. "And another right down the hall." There wasn't a Negro in the South who didn't know the burdens of Jim Crow.

After we'd relieved ourselves and washed up, we followed Mrs. Broussard through her many rooms. There was a living room, a drawing room, two bathrooms, a kitchen, and a dining room just on one floor. We walked into each room through one door and then out of it through another, all the while listening to her talk about her house, which she said was designed and built by her husband, Alonzo, owner of A. L. Broussard and Company, who had built many of the homes in Collier Heights.

"This neighborhood is the first ever designed *by* and *for* our people," Mrs. Broussard told me proudly, as we stood in her large dining room. "The Abernathys live just down the street. The Kings are close by, too. King, *Sr.*," she said, "not Martin and Corey. They're still out in Sweet Auburn. But they come

for dinner often enough. Of course, restaurants in downtown Atlanta don't serve colored people, so we entertain at home. And if you're going to entertain at home, you ought to do it right, is what I say."

I looked around the pretty room with its lush furnishings, which included a large bar cart made of shiny wood with gold hardware, and nodded in agreement, even though I'd never had a dining room myself. The kitchen table where my family ate only seated five, and that was elbow to elbow. If somebody else showed up for supper, we had to bring in a stool off the back porch. The stool *was* sturdy, at least, because if you're going to entertain at home, you ought to do it right, is what I say.

In the kitchen, we met Pearl, the housekeeper, who smiled politely at Mrs. Lucas but barely glanced at me. Then we went through the kitchen door and were somehow back in the hallway.

With all those rooms and doors, I'd lost my sense of direction early on in the tour, but then we walked out onto a large sleeping porch and I figured we were at the back of the house. From there, we entered the house again through a different door, and went down a stairway to a partially underground level, which Mrs. Broussard called the "garden level."

"The pool's over that way," she said, gesturing casually behind us as we turned a corner. "The children spend most of their free time in it. They're excellent swimmers, especially Olivia. She's the best in the eleven- and twelve-year-old group at the club." Looking at me, she said, "Olivia's my oldest. She turned twelve last week. I also have two boys, Alonzo Jr.—he's eight—and Preston—he's six. They're with their grandparents this weekend."

Next, we entered a room whose walls were all shelves lined with books. "This is the library, which you should feel free to enjoy, Doris. Catie told me you were one of the more enthusiastic readers in her class."

"Doris was one of the most engaged students I've ever had," said Mrs. Lucas, from where she was standing by a bookshelf, examining a book: *Their Eyes Were Watching God*. I remembered how she'd loaned me her own copy of that same book, a couple of years earlier. I'd been scandalized, titillated, and absorbed by Janie running off with first one man and then another. The moment I'd finished it, I felt like I'd read something I shouldn't have, something Jesus wouldn't have approved of.

"Well, good for you, hun," Mrs. Broussard said. "But I'm curious why such an enthusiastic and engaged student leaves school."

"My ma's sick," I told her. "So, I stay home to help with my brothers and things 'round the house."

Mrs. Broussard's eyebrow did a little twitch, like she didn't approve of that. "I take it your folks don't know what you're doing here in Atlanta?"

"No, ma'am. They wouldn't allow it."

"You'd think they'd be grateful," she said. "Less time taking care of your own babies gives you more time to take care of theirs."

"Sylvia," Mrs. Lucas said sharply.

Mrs. Broussard looked at her. "What?"

"I . . . don't reckon they'd see it that way," I told her. " 'Sides, taking care of family important, aint it?"

She made a face like she wasn't too sure, like it was a could-be/could-be-not kind of thing. Then she asked, "Well, is it important to you?"

"Yes, ma'am."

"Why?"

It struck me as a ridiculous question and I almost laughed, but her face was serious. I looked over at Mrs. Lucas, but she was still flipping through *Their Eyes Were Watching God* and I couldn't tell if she was listening anymore. "They the people who love me," I said to Mrs. Broussard.

She nodded, but I could tell she wasn't agreeing with me so much as she was thinking it over.

"What is love to you, Doris?" Mrs. Lucas asked, suddenly looking up from the book.

In Mrs. Lucas's class, we used to talk a lot about love, all kinds, in novels and poems and sometimes songs. And I thought enough about love on my own that this was a question I could answer easy. "My folks have always took care of me. Fed me, clothed me, kept a roof over my head, protected me, and told me I was worth something." I felt good about my answer, proud, like I'd aced a test.

"Well, isn't that their job?" Mrs. Broussard asked. "They brought you into this world, didn't they? They're directly responsible for your existence. Or are you the first child in history who asked to be born?"

Never in my seventeen years of life on God's green earth

had anyone ever suggested to me that a child owes nothing to her parents. The Bible says, "Honor thy father and thy mother, that your days may be long upon the land the Lord your God giveth to you," and every pastor, every deacon, every choir director, every good, God-fearing person I'd ever heard speak on the subject, agreed. I stared at Mrs. Broussard, thinking of Pastor Mills, who liked to quote the book of 1 Peter, saying, "Your adversary the devil prowls around like a roaring lion, seeking someone to devour," and I wondered if Mrs. Broussard was really the devil in disguise and I should hightail it back to Millen before she devoured me.

"When I was a child, whenever my mother would tell me she loved me, I'd say, 'I love you, too, Mother.' One day, she told me, 'Sylvie, you don't always have to say that back. It's nice if you love me. But loving me is not your responsibility. All the responsibility in this relationship is mine.' I tell my children the same thing."

What in the blaspheming hell?

"Most people would do well to stop expecting more from their children than they are entitled to expect," she said, with a sharp nod. "Remember that if you ever decide to keep a baby one day."

I glanced toward the door, thought about getting the hell up and away from there, but where would I go? I wasn't about to walk back to Millen, was I? I looked at Mrs. Lucas, expecting to see some sign on her face that she disagreed with all this heathen-talk. But she didn't seem the least bit scandalized.

"Anyway," Mrs. Broussard said, apparently done with blaspheming for the moment, "your appointment with the doctor

is at nine in the morning. His place is only a few miles from here, so Catie can take you on over. If all goes well, you'll be back in time to rest up awhile before lunch. I put you in Dexter's room down the hall."

"Dexter?" I asked, all sorts of discombobulated by this point.

"My no-account step-nephew," she said. "My husband's sister's boy."

I'd never heard the term *step-nephew* before. Far as I knew, a nephew was a nephew, whether by blood or marriage.

"He stays here during the school year," she went on. "Well, he used to. We haven't seen him in a few weeks, since he hocked some of our jewelry and we put him out. Anyway, that room is the quietest, so you'll be able to sleep. Though I doubt you'll be able to. I didn't sleep a wink the night before mine."

"Before your what, ma'am?" I asked. Then I realized. "Oh."

Mrs. Broussard gave me a look like she thought I might be naïve. "You don't think it's only *poor* colored girls who have abortions, do you?"

"No, ma'am." But that's exactly what I'd thought.

"I sat up all night," she said. "I couldn't stop thinking about all the things that could go wrong."

"Syl," Mrs. Lucas said, finally putting the book down. "Don't scare the child."

Mrs. Broussard waved a hand. "Don't worry, Doris. Everything will probably be fine."

Probably? I thought about Miss Janice. It didn't seem fair that I could die trying to get rid of a baby I never asked for in the first place. I felt like crying. I shook my head, trying to keep the tears from coming. "I don't understand why God let this happen."

Mrs. Broussard sort of laughed then, and said, "*God.*"

This was when I *knew* she was a heathen. Not just nervous. Not simply lacking home training. But a *whole heathen,* sure as shit. And, once I realized it, I could see there had been plenty of clues already, besides her strange ideas about parents and children. For starters, there were those pedal pushers she was wearing. A woman in pants wasn't unheard of in 1960, but they weren't very common among the women I knew, especially the ones who went to church. For another thing, she had on red lipstick. Not *red* red. More pinkish-red. But still not a color I'd expect to see on a pious woman, even on a Friday afternoon. And now that I thought about it? That shiny car in the driveway was suspicious, too. You ever seen a soul pull up to Bible study in a convertible?

"Don't you believe in Almighty God, Mrs. Broussard?" I asked.

"I believe in God," she said. "In a way."

In a way? What in the holy name of Jesus was that supposed to mean?

I watched her sweep a lock of hair behind her ear, easy as you please, unbothered at the prospect of burning in the everlasting inferno for her wishy-washy views. Just as I was trying to decide whether I should end my acquaintance with her right there and then, lest I, too, burn in hellfire, she said, "Catie doesn't believe at all."

"Sylvia," Mrs. Lucas said, looking vexed. "For Christ's sake."

For *whose* sake?

Now, listen. It was one thing for this Sylvia Broussard character to be a heathen. But Mrs. Lucas was another matter. Her lipstick was a modest reddish-brown. Her car had a top, like it ought to. She went to church!

"Mrs. Lucas," I said carefully, aware that the world might at any second crumble and fall around me, "you believe in God, don't you?"

She frowned at Mrs. Broussard, sighed, and replied, "This is not a conversation for today," which I took to mean, *No, sugar, I do not.*

I felt hot all of a sudden, itchy under my collar and in my armpits. Mrs. Lucas was the surest thing in my life. At times, over the last few years, she had been the only sure thing. I could lean on her because she was like me—curious, word-loving—and she was constant. I knew her. I could've sworn I did.

"Doris? Are you alright?" Mrs. Lucas asked. She sounded concerned, no doubt because I was suddenly short of breath, and sweating like a loose woman at Sunday service. "Sit down, Doris," she said, steering me toward a chair. I half-sat, half-collapsed onto it.

"Get her some water, would you, Syl?"

Mrs. Broussard rolled her eyes. I could tell she thought I was being overdramatic. But she went to the door and called upstairs to Pearl to bring a cool glass of water.

Mrs. Lucas held my hand, patting it gently, until Pearl arrived with the water. When she saw me, she looked concerned, too. "What's happened to the poor child?" she asked. Then, peering at me, "You look like you seen a ghost."

"No," Mrs. Broussard said, "just an atheist."

Pearl frowned and I felt relieved. At least I wasn't the only believer around here. But then I realized I couldn't be sure she was frowning at atheism itself, and not at me for having to be brought a glass of water at the mere idea of atheism. Either way, she handed me the glass, then turned and went back upstairs without another word.

"Maybe you should lie down until dinner," Mrs. Broussard said.

Mrs. Lucas nodded. "That's a good idea."

"Dinner's at seven," Mrs. Broussard said. "Alonzo will join us. I told him y'all were coming but I didn't say why." Addressing me, she said, "I'll introduce you as Catie's niece."

"Yes, ma'am."

"He's leaving for Memphis tonight, so he won't be around for the party, of course."

"What party?" Mrs. Lucas asked.

"Oh, did I forget to mention it? I'm having a little get-together tomorrow night."

Mrs. Lucas looked bothered by this news. "Who's going to be at this little get-together? The Kings? The Abernathys?"

Mrs. Broussard sort of chuckled. "It's not that kind of party, Catie."

Mrs. Lucas looked even more bothered now. "I never would have brought Doris here if I knew you were having a party, Sylvia."

Mrs. Broussard peered at Mrs. Lucas for a moment, like she couldn't figure out what the big deal was. But then a look of understanding came over her face. "Well, I guess I didn't think it through all the way."

"Didn't think it . . . ?" Mrs. Lucas's words trailed off. She shook her head in disbelief.

"Listen, Catie," Mrs. Broussard said, with just a pinch of sharpness in her voice. "I'm sorry, alright? I didn't even think you'd really come."

"Stop saying that."

"Why?" Mrs. Broussard asked. "Would you rather not be reminded that you hadn't spoken a word to me for two years before you called asking for a favor? And a big one at that?"

Something like guilt flashed in Mrs. Lucas's eyes. I remembered what she'd said back in Millen, about it being "complicated" to call Mrs. Broussard for help. Seemed like they'd fallen out. It must've been a bad fight, I thought, if Mrs. Broussard was still mad enough to take her to task for it two years after the fact, and in front of a stranger, no less. My cheeks burned with secondhand embarrassment for Mrs. Lucas. But she looked at me and smiled, calm as always. "Let's get you to your room, alright, Doris?"

My room was on the garden level, and like all the rooms in Mrs. Broussard's house, it was big. It was bright, with a row of windows looking out on a flower garden, where petunias, sunkissed yellow and wine-red, were tucked in beside Shasta daisies and baby's breath. Another row of windows looked out on a brick patio at the back of the house. I could see an outdoor dining table and chairs, made of wrought iron, and a shiny, silver barbecue grill standing in a corner. In the bedroom, there was a big bed, a record player that looked brand-new, and there was an attached bathroom. "I think we ought to leave on Saturday, right after you've seen the doctor," Mrs. Lucas said.

"Just on account of a party?" I asked. "What the big fuss about it?"

"Well, Sylvia's friends are . . ." She seemed to struggle finding the right word. "A little wild. Or they used to be, anyway. They used to like to get skunk-drunk and dance half naked and howl at the moon."

Skunk-drunk was a term I knew. Ma was fond of using it to describe the level of inebriation that would cause someone to fall sideways off a porch in the middle of telling a story, or forget to pull up their pants after leaving the outhouse, if they made it to the outhouse at all. Heathens got *skunk-drunk.* My uncle Al had been *skunk-drunk* when his wife caught him getting a head job in a whorehouse. I knew I should stay away from anybody aint have the self-control to quit imbibing before they reached *skunk-drunkness.* On the other hand, for all I knew, Ma's definition of *skunk-drunk* was different from Mrs. Lucas's. Millen folk are different from Atlanta folk. Rich folk are different from poor folk. Rich folk never forget to pull up their pants coming out of outhouses, because rich folk have indoor plumbing. When I squinted at it just the right way, it seemed possible that rich, skunk-drunk Atlantans were only as wild as tipsy Millen bums, and I'd seen more than one of them half naked and howling in public before I was seven years old. Maybe the Good Lord wanted me to stay away from skunk-drunk Atlantans, or maybe he wasn't all that troubled about it either way. How would I ever know for sure if we went home before the party? But Mrs. Lucas was fluffing a pillow and saying, "You can rest at my house until Sunday."

"But what if I aint feeling well?" I asked her. "What if something go wrong and I need the doctor?"

She sighed.

"I'll stay in the bed," I told her. "I won't even go upstairs. I probably won't feel up to it, no way." The best lies have some truth in them. It *was* possible, even more like than not, that I wouldn't feel up for the party, and that made me feel less bad about the fact that I would otherwise try to sneak on in. I wanted to know what a rich-Negro party was like. In the photographs of celebrity shindigs in *Jet* magazine, there was always champagne, elegant clothing, and vases full of white flowers everywhere. Most of the parties I'd been to were church events, or birthday parties. Last year, I'd convinced Ma and Daddy to let me go to Lena's sweet sixteen, even though they knew there was like to be dancing to the devil's music, which there was, along with plenty more scandalous behavior on top of that. It was a good time, right on. But none of the parties I'd been to were anything close to *fancy*, and I wanted to see what one was like.

"Alright, Doris," Mrs. Lucas replied. "As long as you stay in your room."

She fluffed the pillow some more and then stood back from

the bed and smiled at me. I lay down, and spent a minute getting myself comfortable on the bed. While I tried to find just the right position, I asked Mrs. Lucas something I'd been wondering. "Why would somebody rich as Mrs. Broussard get rid of a baby?"

"Some women don't want more children, or any children at all, even if they can afford them," Mrs. Lucas said.

"That's sinful. Any woman who'd do that, when she aint have to, ought to burn in hellfire." It was a bold statement. I can see that now. But when you're young, you think you know every damn thing. Mrs. Lucas just looked at me curiously, her head tilted to one side in that way she had.

"But I reckon you don't believe in hell," I said, "if you don't believe in God."

"I don't believe in God the way you do, Doris," she told me, "the way church folks do. But I do believe in the possibility of a power greater than myself."

This sounded like more blaspheming to me, but for years I'd hung on Mrs. Lucas's every word, and I wasn't ready to quit her brain cold turkey, heathen or not, so I let her go on.

"And if there is such a power," she said, "I don't believe it cares whether you have an abortion at all, let alone send you, or Sylvia, or any other woman, to 'hell' for it. I'd think a higher power would have better things to worry about."

"Like what?" I could think of plenty better things for the Good Lord to dwell on, but I wanted to know what she thought.

"Keeping the Earth suspended in the cosmos, for one thing. That all by itself must require a great deal of concentration."

I suddenly remembered a conversation I'd had with Daddy when I was about eight. I'd heard some women from church talking about another woman who'd recently shown up to Bible study in a skirt without a slip under it, greatly offending the Almighty, according to them. I thought if that was true, then the Lord must be real petty. What else would you call a God who got his own drawers in a twist over some woman's underwear? But Daddy said God needed women to be modest, to help men control themselves. I asked, if God had created men in his image, did that mean God had problems controlling his own self? Daddy had reminded me not to blaspheme, lest I burn in hell for it, so I pushed all those thoughts away. Now I wondered if I'd been right all along.

"Religious people's ideas of God have always felt small to me," Mrs. Lucas said. "I can't fathom a God caring about what people do, whatever they do, for whatever reasons. What would be a *valid* excuse for ending a pregnancy, according to your God?"

"If the woman got forced. Or it was incest," I said, without having to think about it. Those were the big ones that most folks agreed on. "Maybe if you know the baby gon' be sickly and die early, or just be in pain and miserable all its life. That's it, I reckon. Anything else selfish."

"Is it never okay to be selfish?" Mrs. Lucas asked.

I opened my mouth to say no, but then closed it, because I wasn't sure.

Mrs. Lucas patted my hand, smiled reassuringly, and turned to the door.

"Have you ever had one?" I asked her.

She looked back at me. "No, I haven't," she said.

After she left, I leaned back on the fluffed-up pillows and sighed. I almost wished she *had* had an abortion, so I could've asked her how much it would hurt.

4

I woke up an hour later from a restless, dreamless sleep, to the faint smells of cooking food and the sounds of music drifting down to me from upstairs. I lay there for a few minutes, listening to the song—a jazz tune I'd never heard. It was slow, melancholy, and it made me feel like crying. I already had enough to cry about without adding a song to the mix, and if I started crying about all of that I might never stop, so I got out of bed and went to wash up.

I'd never slept in a bedroom with its own bathroom before. I hovered at the doorway this time, looking in, wondering how people with money decided what to spend it on. How had the Broussards decided how many bathrooms they needed in this house? Was there some kind of special math to figure out how many different toilets a rich Negro needed to piss in, in order to feel truly free?

The bathroom was almost as big as the bedroom. Almost everything in it, including all the fixtures and wall tile, was pale yellow, except for some tile that was trimmed along the top and bottom in aqua blue. That blue was matched in the plaid wallpaper, and in the floor tile, which was checkered yellow and aqua. Every inch of the room was pristine. It didn't smell like a bathroom at all, had no real odors of any kind, except the very faint scent of Camay soap.

I washed up, combed my hair, and changed into the best dress I'd brought with me, which was dark blue with white polka dots. I didn't think the dress was good enough for fancy dinner in a fancy house like this, but it was the best I could do.

Even though Mrs. Broussard had given us a tour of her house, when I stepped out of my room I didn't know where to go. I walked down a hallway and found myself back in the library. I went back the other way and found a flight of stairs. I went up, and came into another hallway and, following the smell of food, came to the kitchen, where Pearl was humming along to another jazz tune, while slicing tomatoes.

"'Scuse me, ma'am," I said.

She looked up at me, eyebrows raised.

"My auntie here?"

"They in the drawing room," she said, nodding toward a doorway.

"Thank you," I said, and started that way, before stopping to ask, "Ma'am? What's a drawing room for?"

"Drinking and talking, mostly," Pearl said. "Sometime they read in there."

"They don't drink and talk and read in all these other rooms?"

"They do," she said. "But the drawing room more private. It aint a place for, say, party guests. Only family and close friends."

"But nobody go in there to draw, I reckon? So, why they call it that?"

"Chile," she said, amused, "your guess good as mine."

I didn't need to find the drawing room, because right then Mrs. Lucas and Mrs. Broussard came in the kitchen.

"Doris," Mrs. Lucas said when she saw me, "how you feeling?"

"Much better, ma'am."

"Well, you're just in time for dinner," said Mrs. Broussard. "Isn't she, Pearl?"

Pearl nodded. "I'm just finishing up the salad."

"Well, let's get these on the table." Mrs. Broussard moved to the counter and picked up a tray with a roasted chicken on it. "Catie, grab the greens, would you? Doris, bring the sweet potatoes."

Mrs. Lucas got the collards, and I got the sweet potatoes, and we all carried the food into the dining room and placed it on the table, which was set with pretty, cream-colored plates, shiny silverware, and drinking glasses so clear they almost weren't there. Pearl followed with the salad and bread, and then disappeared into the kitchen again.

"Alonzo won't be joining us after all," Mrs. Broussard said, taking her seat at one end of the table. Mrs. Lucas and I sat down on either side of her. "He's working late, as always." She didn't say it like it bothered her, more like it was just a simple fact of life. "The company's finishing up construction on four new houses this week."

There was an extra fork at each place setting, and I had no idea why. I watched Mrs. Lucas and Mrs. Broussard to see what they did, then mimicked them, using the outside fork for the salad, which had tomatoes so dark red they were almost purple, and cucumbers cut in cubes instead of sliced. I couldn't see any dressing on the salad, but I could taste some, a creamy lemon flavor that I might've liked if I hadn't been a little queasy still. As it was, all I could do was pick at the food and push it around on my plate, hoping Mrs. Broussard wasn't studying me, or that she wouldn't be offended if she was. I got distracted thinking about how many bites I could take without throwing up, and when I tuned back in to the conversation, Mrs. Broussard was saying, "You know who we just built a house for, two streets over? Scooter Douglas. You remember him? His sister, Frances, was in the Bobby Socks with us."

Mrs. Lucas chewed slowly and thought about it. "The one whose family moved to Richmond?"

"No, that's Scooter Brown. Scooter Douglas's family moved to Newark."

"Oh, Big Scooter."

"That's right. He just moved back to Atlanta and he's bigger than ever. He's an attorney. Can you believe it? With the stutter he used to have?"

I wanted to know what "the Bobby Socks" was, but I felt shy to ask. Something about being in that big house made me feel small. But Mrs. Lucas must've seen in my face that I was lost in the conversation, because she said, "The Bobby Socks was a social club. For young people." I appreciated her trying, but it didn't really help me understand because the idea of "a social club for young people" just wasn't something I could wrap my head around. We had clubs at school, and at church, for kids who like science or reading the Bible, say. And young folks did socialize at those clubs, right on. But a club *just* for socializing? All by itself? It didn't sound right. But I nodded along anyhow, not wanting to seem like a rube.

"Catie and I met in the Bobby Socks when we were five years old," Mrs. Broussard said. "I still remember the first time I saw her, in a sailor dress with knee socks, sitting in a corner with her nose in a book. It was a party, you know, we were supposed to be dancing or talking to each other, but there she sat, reading *Tender Is the Night* or whatever it was."

"Oh, for goodness' sake," Mrs. Lucas said. "It wasn't *Tender Is the Night.* What five-year-old you know reads F. Scott Fitzgerald?"

"What five-year-old reads a book at a party at all?" Mrs. Broussard asked.

"It *wasn't* a book. It was a pamphlet about polio that someone on the street handed us on the way over. You know this, Sylvia. I've told you a hundred times."

Mrs. Broussard shrugged. "My version's better. It captures your bookish spirit."

"My 'bookish spirit' had nothing to do with it," Mrs. Lucas said, looking at me now. "I was just feeling shy and trying to avoid mingling."

I wondered what the hell kind of party for five-year-olds had them up in there *mingling.* All the parties I'd been at with kids that age was just a whole bunch of screaming and pushing and sticky handprints everywhere. I tried to picture these two grown women as small children, mingling with each other. It was a strain on my imagination. Mrs. Lucas was thirty-four—

which I knew because I'd seen her driver's license once, a couple of years before—so Mrs. Broussard must've been, too. Mrs. Lucas was the sort of woman who seemed born into adulthood, so mature—so smart, so capable—that it seemed possible she came into being in this very form, appearing out of a thick puff of smoke, like the good witch in *The Wizard of Oz.* I didn't know Mrs. Broussard enough to say how mature she was, but I couldn't imagine her as a mingling kindergartner, either. A gum-popping ten-year-old was about all I could manage, and even that took a whole lot of squinting.

"Well, whatever the reading material was," Mrs. Broussard said, "I walked right up and snatched it out of her hand. And I put *my* hand on my hip, like this, and I said, 'I'm Sylvia Ruffin, and I'm the best at dancing the Charleston. You gonna dance with me?' And she sort of stared at me, like she was trying to figure out who raised me."

"I assumed it was jackals."

"And she said—and I'll never forget this—she said, 'If your Charleston is as pushy as your so-called friendship, I don't think I can handle it.'" Mrs. Broussard laughed and shook her head. "You ever hear a five-year-old talk like that?"

I couldn't answer because I was dwelling on the fact that five-year-olds also danced the Charleston at this party. Atlanta Negroes really were something else.

Mrs. Lucas frowned at Mrs. Broussard. "For Christ's sake. Five-year-olds don't talk like that, Sylvia."

"Well, maybe I'm embellishing a bit. But you get my point, don't you, Doris? She was sharp, is what I'm saying. The sharpest little girl I'd ever met. I knew I had to be friends with a girl like that."

"I'm flattered you remember me that way," Mrs. Lucas said. Then she looked at me. "I bet Doris was like that, too. A sharp mind at five wouldn't surprise me one bit."

The compliment made my cheeks warm. That was the thing about Mrs. Lucas. She could see things about you that other people sometimes couldn't, that most people didn't look long enough to notice. She saw these things, and when you looked at her, you saw them reflecting back at you.

"Well, aren't you two peas in a pod," Mrs. Broussard said, and I thought maybe I heard a rough edge in her tone, even though she was smiling. I looked at Mrs. Lucas, to see if she'd noticed it, but if she had, she wasn't letting on.

Mrs. Broussard took a bite of sweet potato, chewed it slowly, then changed the subject. "What y'all think about the sit-ins?" she asked. "I, for one, was hoping the students would forget about all that nonsense over the summer, but now they're back and I hear they're getting started up again."

"You should've known they would," Mrs. Lucas said. "Young people are on fire down here."

"'On fire' is exactly what they are," Mrs. Broussard replied. "A raging, out-of-control fire about to burn down everything we've built."

Back in Millen, I hadn't thought too much about the movement, mostly because there was no movement back in Millen. I only heard about the lunch-counter sit-ins through word of mouth and an article I'd read back in February, when the demonstrations had started out in Greensboro, North Carolina. Daddy brought home a copy of the *Daily World* that somebody had brought back from Atlanta and left at the shop where he worked. Our town didn't have a colored newspaper, and Daddy told me the local white paper hadn't mentioned the Greensboro demonstrations at all. But when the sit-ins had spread, from North Carolina all over the South, even *The Millen News* couldn't ignore them anymore. They ran a few very short articles, about this or other sit-in in a diner in Nashville, or a department store lunch counter in Jacksonville, or wherever colored folks were getting up to such things that week. I knew these articles existed because I heard people talking about them, but I never read them. The whole to-do seemed so far away.

"Colored people have come a long way since the plantation," Mrs. Broussard said. "We're doctors and architects now. Even stuttering Scooter is a damn lawyer! It hasn't been easy, but we've started to see what's possible if we work hard and stick together."

"That's easy for you to say, Syl," Mrs. Lucas replied. "You and Alonzo have a lot more than most colored people."

"We sit on the board of the NAACP," said Mrs. Broussard, "and plenty of other organizations, and we give generously, I promise you. Listen, I'm not saying the problems of colored people have all been solved, not by a long shot, but we're getting there, slowly but surely, of our own volition. All this integration nonsense is just rocking the boat. Besides, I don't understand why anyone would *want* to eat lunch beside people who despise them. I wouldn't be able to get a bite down."

She sounded like Daddy. He was born five years after the 1919 race riots in Jenkins County, when mobs of white men had roamed Millen and surrounding towns, murdering colored people and burning down churches. His ma and daddy had been there when the riots happened, and had fled to Philadelphia soon after. But they'd returned to Millen two years later. Philadelphia was too cold in too many ways, and I reckon they missed home and family more than they didn't miss fear. So Daddy was born in Millen, and was brought up connected to that same home and family. And that same fear. He raised me and my brothers to believe that all whites were dangerous, every last one of them to one degree or another, and to stay as far away from them as we could. Daddy didn't believe in integration. He thought any plan to get closer to whites was a suicide mission. He believed in activism for better jobs and better housing, not desegregation of lunch. So, when he heard about the sit-ins, he responded the way he always did to any news of social-integration-related protest: He mumbled, "These niggers done lost they fool minds," and spit tobacco juice on the ground. After some nudging, he went on: "Aint no sense under heaven getting your brains beat out so you can eat a meal next to white people. These young folk going to college, getting education. That already more than most of us can do." He shook his head. "Nobody grateful for what they got no more."

I reckoned Daddy felt that way because of his fear and distrust of whites, which made plenty sense to me. I also saw it as the opinion of a man who'd never had much of anything, and carried deep within him the knowledge that what little he did have could be ripped away at any moment, so he should be thankful to the Lord and never get greedy. But Mrs. Broussard didn't strike me as a *be grateful for what you got and don't get greedy* kind of person, so I was surprised to hear her talk about the sit-ins the same way Daddy did. To tell the truth, it confused me. I knew older Negroes liked to move slow. It was a known fact in 1960 that eighty percent of Negroes over thirty thought molasses ran too quick. I reckoned that was why it took us over four hundred years to get out of slavery: Negroes over thirty shaking their heads at Harriet Tubman, mumbling about gratitude while spitting tobacco juice. Still, I agreed with Daddy and Mrs. Broussard both, far as I had an opinion at all, which I mostly didn't, because I knew no matter how many lunch counters were desegregated in Atlanta or Greensboro, the white folks in Millen, Jenkins County, Georgia, weren't about to sip coffee or eat sandwiches next to a Negro, no matter what the law told them. And, ignorant though I was about the whole thing, I still reckoned Daddy was right about being thankful for what you had. The Bible says to give thanks in all circumstances. Jesus don't like ingratitude.

"I don't think eating beside them is the point, Syl," Mrs. Lucas said.

"Well, what's the point, then? You tell me, Catie, because I swear I don't know."

"The point is not wanting to be second-class citizens anymore. We can shop in downtown Atlanta but if we need the bathroom, we either have to hold it until we get home or use one of the colored-only restrooms no one ever bothers to clean. And choosing where we eat or don't eat is a different thing than *being told* where we can eat or not, which I'm sure you *do* know.

I support desegregation, of lunch counters and everything else. *Integration* is obviously another matter."

"What's the difference?" I asked her.

"Desegregation is what they put in the law," Mrs. Lucas told me. "Desegregating lunch counters means colored people have a legal right to be served. It doesn't mean we'll always choose to eat there."

"Why won't we?"

"Well, we might," she said. "But then what will happen to *our* restaurants, the ones *owned* by colored people, where we eat now? Where we're already welcome to sit and stay as long as we please? Where we've never had to feel like second-class citizens?"

There were two sit-down restaurants owned by colored people in Millen. I'd eaten in only one of them, a place called Edie Griffin's, where Daddy took me for lunch when I turned sixteen, and again on my seventeenth birthday.

"Why can't we have both?" I asked Mrs. Lucas. "Why can't we eat in they restaurants and ours?"

"Maybe we can," she said. "But the Magnolia Room at Rich's Department Store downtown has been there since I was a child. And the store itself has been around, in one location or another, for a hundred years. There are no hundred-year-old colored businesses. We were still being bought and sold ourselves a hundred years ago. So, if we can have both, fine. But if we can't? Which do you think will be lost?"

I didn't know anything about the Magnolia Room, or Rich's Department Store, but I understood her point. It was the first time I'd thought about integration hurting colored businesses, and the first time I'd heard Mrs. Lucas talk about it, either. This sit-in movement, the one spreading across the South in 1960, hadn't even begun when I was still in school, but there had been some talk around Millen about the Katz Drug Store sit-in over in Oklahoma City in 1958. When somebody brought it up during English, Mrs. Lucas had asked us what we thought. One or two of my classmates insisted it was foolishness, but a lot of them were for it. I didn't know much about it, so I kept quiet. And, I realized now, Mrs. Lucas hadn't ever said what *she* thought.

"Young people these days don't value community the way we did," Mrs. Broussard was saying. "Y'all want the whole world."

I wanted to ask her who this "y'all" was but I didn't want to be disrespectful. I didn't want the world. Why would I? The world hadn't ever felt like something I could get.

"Y'all want to give up everything we've built," Mrs. Broussard went on. "And for what? To eat and pray and go to school with white folks? That's another one that makes my ass itch. *School integration.* What kind of fool nonsense? Don't y'all know school integration will be the end of colored teachers?"

I looked at Mrs. Lucas, who nodded. "I can't see white administrators hiring colored teachers."

"And what will be the impact," Mrs. Broussard asked, "of white teachers on colored children? Nothing good, that's what. You think a white teacher would be helping you now the way Catie is, risking jail for you?"

"*Jail?*" Mrs. Lucas sounded amused. "You think the law gives a damn if there's one less colored baby in Jenkins County?

White doctors take out our uteruses when we go in for minor surgery, for God's sake."

I tried not to wince at her taking the Lord's name in vain.

"Alright. Not jail, then," Mrs. Broussard allowed. "But you could lose your job, Catie. Your standing in your community."

"*My* standing?" Mrs. Lucas asked. "What about yours, Syl? You're helping us, aren't you?"

Mrs. Broussard waved the notion away. "I don't have a job to worry about, and my standing in the community is always at risk."

I wondered what she meant by that. It seemed rude to ask.

"No one's going to find out," Mrs. Lucas said, sounding sure. "Women end pregnancies all the time. The lucky ones always have help and we don't hear anything about it. Why are you being so dramatic all of a sudden?"

"I guess I just worry about you," Mrs. Broussard replied.

"Don't worry about me. Worry about Doris."

Out the corner of my eye, I thought I saw someone walk past the dining room. Mrs. Broussard saw them, too. She stood up and called out, "Alonzo!"

A moment later, the man from the painting in the front hall entered.

"What are you doing here?" she asked him, surprised. "I thought you were working late."

He was dressed like a rich Negro, in a very sharp blue suit and expensive-looking shoes. He looked just like the painting of himself—hazel eyes, thin mustache, high-yellow enough to pass for white if he wanted to—only he was much shorter, half a foot shorter than his wife, at least.

"I was, and now I'm running late for the train to Memphis," he said, as she leaned down a little so he could kiss her on the cheek. "I just came to grab the suitcase I somehow left behind this morning." He looked at Mrs. Lucas, gave her a tight-lipped smile. It was the kind of smile you give somebody who keeps beating you at cards. They aint cheating, so you got no cause to be rude, but no, you *don't* want to play one more hand, thank you very much. "Evening, Cate," he said.

"Evening, Alonzo," she replied, with more warmth in her voice than he had in his.

"How you been?" he asked.

"I've been well, thank you."

He looked at me. "Who's this young lady?" he asked, his smile easier now.

"You remember Catie's niece, don't you?" Mrs. Broussard asked him.

He nodded slowly. "Of course I do. Uh . . ."

"Doris," I said.

"That's it. Look at you, all grown up."

"Yes, sir."

Mrs. Broussard winked at me, and it was all I could do not to laugh.

"Well, I better get my bag and get on out of here," he said to his wife. "Have fun this weekend. But not *too much* fun." I could've sworn his eyes darted toward Mrs. Lucas when he said that last part.

"Same to you," Mrs. Broussard said.

"Nice to see you, Doris. And you, Cate."

He kissed Mrs. Broussard on the cheek again and left, his

expensive shoes clicking along the hallway to the back of the house.

"You'll have to excuse my husband," Mrs. Broussard said to me once he was gone. "He's usually very friendly. But he always gets in a mood when Catie's around."

I opened my mouth to ask why, but then Mrs. Lucas said, "Sylvia," in a tone sharp as a blade, and I shut it.

5

hen Mrs. Lucas said she wanted to go to bed early, Mrs. Broussard was offended. "It's barely eight o'clock!"

"We have to get up early."

"Not *that* early," Mrs. Broussard replied. "Have a drink, at least. I have a bottle of rum I think you'll like. Doris, you want a Coke?"

Pearl was washing dishes, so Mrs. Broussard went to the kitchen and got a Coke for me, and then Mrs. Lucas and I followed her to the drawing room. Pearl was right about it being more private. It was tucked behind the dining room in a way that you wouldn't have been able to find it unless you knew it was there. It was homey, with walls painted a rich, warm green, and soft couches and chairs. There was a liquor cabinet built into one wall, and a large fireplace that had a fire blazing in it, which I guessed Pearl must've got going. Above the mantel was another large portrait of the Broussard family, holding hands, smiling, looking happy and rich.

Mrs. Broussard went over to the liquor cabinet and got out three pretty glasses. In each glass, she placed ice from a fancy little bucket. She poured rum in two of the glasses, and Coke in the third, and handed one each to me and Mrs. Lucas, who looked surprised as Mrs. Broussard raised the other glass to her own lips.

"Since when are you drinking again?" Mrs. Lucas asked.

"Oh," Mrs. Broussard said, looking at the glass, like she hadn't expected the question. "Since a couple of years ago, I guess."

Mrs. Lucas frowned.

"It's fine, Catie. It's *been* fine. I promise." She held up the glass. "Let's have a toast. To old friends," she said, and then, looking at me, "and new."

I smiled and raised my Coke in her direction. Mrs. Broussard clinked her glass against Mrs. Lucas's and right then the doorbell rang. A few moments later, there were voices out in the hall, and then a woman came into the drawing room, a pregnant woman I thought looked a whole lot like Coretta Scott King.

Mrs. Broussard hurried over to her, opening her arms wide. "Coretta!" she said, and I almost shit.

"Sylvia, I hope you don't mind us dropping in so unexpected," Mrs. King said.

"Mind? Of course not! I'm thrilled to see you."

"We were just over at the Abernathys for dinner, and we wanted to stop in and say hello before heading back downtown."

"You and Martin?"

"Oh, no," said Mrs. King. "Martin's off doing Martin things. Julia's with me."

"Well, this is a wonderful surprise," Mrs. Broussard said, sounding excited.

"Is that Cate Lucas?" Mrs. King said when she saw her, and rushed over.

"Coretta!" Mrs. Lucas smiled brightly as they embraced.

I just stood there staring. What else could I do?

"My goodness, how long has it been?"

"Three years at least," Mrs. Lucas said. "And look at you. Congratulations!" She placed her hand on Mrs. King's swollen belly.

Without thinking, I placed my hand on mine.

"I ran into your mother just yesterday," Mrs. King said. "She didn't tell me you were in town."

"She doesn't know," Mrs. Lucas replied. "No one knows. We only got here today and I'm not sure I'll have time to drop in on them before we go."

"Well, then, I never saw you," Mrs. King said.

There was another voice in the hallway then, a distinct, scratchy sort of voice, saying, "Only if it's no trouble, alright, Pearl?" And then the owner of the voice appeared in the doorway. I almost dropped my Coke. Right there, standing not ten feet from me, was Mrs. King's even more famous cousin, the singer Julia Avery.

She was taller than she looked in magazines, and her brown skin had a peachy tone to it that no photo I ever saw of her, before or since, really captured. She wasn't exactly pretty, in photos or in real life, but the same confidence and self-possession that jumped off every image of her seemed to vibrate from her skin now, as she stood in the doorway. She was dressed in a black pencil skirt and a white sweater with a neckline low enough to make the Almighty blush.

"Look what the cat dragged in!" Mrs. Broussard hollered when she saw her. "I thought you'd gone back to Memphis!"

"If only," Julia Avery replied, and they hugged.

When they parted, she noticed me. I was hard to miss, standing there staring, my mouth open wide enough to drive Mrs. Broussard's Studebaker into it. Julia Avery didn't smile at me, she just sort of looked me over.

"This is Doris," Mrs. Broussard said. "Catie's niece."

I thought I saw a flash of confusion on her face, but it was gone quick, replaced by something else: eagerness, as she turned to look for Mrs. Lucas. When she saw her, still standing by the liquor cabinet with Mrs. King, she finally did smile. "*Cate,*" she said, and the name was like a lyric coming out of her mouth, sung more than said, lifting like a melody into the air. "I didn't know you were in Atlanta."

A memory came to me, all of a sudden. A couple of years before, there'd been a rumor that Julia Avery had been spotted in Millen, driving down Statesboro in a fancy car. I hadn't believed it, because no one I knew claimed to have seen her with their own eyes. Everybody heard about it from somebody else. This was all about a week after Mrs. Lucas's husband died, and when Sister Paulette, the choir director at our church, said she heard Julia Avery had been at the repast after the funeral, I'd thought it was some fool nonsense for sure. I'd been at the funeral, along with most everybody else in town, and Julia Avery sure hadn't been there. In the years since, I'd forgot all about the rumor. And now here Julia Avery was, calling Mrs. Lucas by her Christian name.

Her long legs carried her across the room in three strides, and then she was reaching out for Mrs. Lucas's hand. I saw her own hand was studded with rings, one of them a sparkly diamond. I watched it catch the light as Mrs. Lucas's hand slipped easily into hers. "We only arrived this evening," Mrs. Lucas said.

"How you been?" Julia Avery asked.

"Fair to middlin'. But I can't complain. How are *you*?" Mrs. Lucas asked, her tone suddenly more serious.

"You know me, Cate. I never really know how I'm doing until it's too late."

A few weeks before, I'd read an article in *Jet* magazine that said she was in the hospital, suffering from exhaustion, which I hadn't even known was a thing you could be hospitalized for. Half the women I knew seemed exhausted all the time.

"I got the book you sent," she continued, "and the flowers. Thank you."

"You look good," Mrs. Lucas said.

"Well, that's a goddamn lie. But I do appreciate the kindness. *You* look good, though. Fine as ever," she said, and pulled Mrs. Lucas close, slipping her arms around her waist in a way I'd only ever seen men hang on to women. I noticed it, and I must have thought it was strange, but I didn't dwell on it because everything about that moment was strange.

Mrs. Lucas quickly removed Julia Avery's arms from

around her waist and took a step back, nodding in my direction. "Have you met my niece?"

She looked me over again. "Doris, was it?"

"Yes, ma'am."

She scoffed. "Ma'am? Do I look like somebody's mama to you, child?"

I wasn't sure how to answer that. She looked old enough to be somebody's mama, right on. But nobody's mama I knew showed that much cleavage.

"Call me Julia, alright?"

"Yes, ma'am. Yes, Miss Julia."

I was about to ask how they knew each other, but Mrs. King put her hand on Mrs. Lucas's arm and said, "Cate, I want to apologize again for missing Robert's funeral."

Mrs. Lucas shook her head. "There's nothing to apologize for. Your husband was stabbed, for goodness' sake. I didn't take it personally. I appreciated your letter and the flowers."

"Speaking of your husband," Mrs. Broussard said to Mrs. King, "we were just talking about the sit-ins."

"That's Snick," Mrs. King replied, "not SCLC."

"Well, close enough," said Mrs. Broussard.

Mrs. King scoffed. "Don't let the students hear you say that." Then she waved a hand. "Anyway, I get enough of this talk at home. And at church. And everywhere else I go. So, let's talk about something else."

"Y'all want a drink?"

"A quick one," Mrs. King replied. "We can only stay a minute."

• • •

Two rounds of rum and an hour and some later, they were still there. I'd learned that Mrs. Lucas and Julia Avery had known each other since they were students at Spelman. I couldn't believe Mrs. Lucas never mentioned it. If I was friends with anybody as famous as Julia Avery, you wouldn't be able to shut me up about it.

I watched Mrs. Lucas, sitting on a couch between Miss Julia and Mrs. Broussard, talking and laughing with her friends. She looked so different. Her shoes were off, and she was curled up, with her arms wrapped around her knees. She'd taken off her sweater and her arms were bare. A lock of hair had come undone from the pins in her updo, and she hadn't bothered to put it back. This was the closest to disheveled I'd ever seen her. But her eyes were so bright.

Miss Julia was telling me and Mrs. Lucas how she'd ended up in the hospital, a story Mrs. Broussard and Mrs. King already knew. It had all started, she said, during one of her shows. "I was onstage down at the Royal Peacock, singing 'Stormy Weather'—"

"My favorite," Mrs. King interrupted.

Julia nodded. "I know it is, cousin, that's why I always think of you when I sing it. Anyhow, I was right around 'gloom and misery everywhere' when I started to feel woozy. I was trying to think how to get to the stool and sit down without it looking obvious, and next thing I know, I'm waking up in the hospital! The first thing I said to the nurse was, 'Sugar, let me out of here, I got to get back to the show!' She said, 'My dear, the show was two days ago!' I'd been asleep *two days*!"

"What did they say was wrong?" Mrs. Lucas asked.

"My blood pressure, for one thing. It was sky high. My thyroid wasn't acting right, either. And I'd hardly been sleeping besides. They kept me there for a week. Then when they let me out, they said I wasn't to travel. They told me to stop smoking," she said, raising her lit cigarette, "and quit drinking while I was at it," she continued, raising her glass of rum. "So, I spent a couple weeks wearing out my welcome at Coretta's before I moved over to the Royal Hotel."

Mrs. King waved a hand. "Oh, stop it. You know I loved having you. It always reminds me of when I used to come visit you at school, and we'd stay up late talking."

"I was just thinking the other day, about that time we smoked that scary reefer," Mrs. Broussard said.

"*Which* time?" Miss Julia asked.

"The time Coretta came down for homecoming," said Mrs. Broussard. "Junior year."

"Oh, you mean that shit we got from those Atlanta University boys!" Miss Julia said.

"What on earth are y'all talking about?" Mrs. Lucas asked.

Mrs. Broussard looked shocked. "Catie, don't tell me you forgot this!"

"She probably blocked it out," Mrs. King said, laughing.

Miss Julia shook her head in disappointment. "Catherine Olivia Boatwright, don't tell me you're too siddity to admit to getting high as a kite and running through Morehouse North in your bloomers."

I stared wide-eyed at Mrs. Lucas. "You did that?"

"We all did it," Miss Julia said. "Well, not Sylvia. She stripped buck-ass naked."

Mrs. Broussard cackled. "Our dorm mother was in hysterics!"

They all fell out laughing then, and I laughed with them.

"Talking about hysterics," Mrs. King said, once the laughter had died down, "we ought to get back to Sweet Auburn before one of my children wakes up and realizes I'm gone. Or, worse, my husband."

I stood by the front door while they all said their good nights. Through the screen door, I could see a man out on the porch, standing under the light, tall and broad shouldered in a dark suit, just standing there looking out at the road, a serious look on his face. Somehow I knew he was there to protect Mrs. King.

Mrs. Broussard invited Mrs. King and her husband for dinner late the following week, and Mrs. King said they'd be delighted. "You're invited, too, Julia," Mrs. Broussard said.

"Thanks, Syl, but I'm finally headed home to Memphis on Sunday, and then back on the road next week."

"Well, come to my party tomorrow. I'd have invited you already if I'd known you were still in town."

"Will you be there, Cate?" Miss Julia asked, looking hopeful.

"I suppose so."

"Well, alright. Sounds like a good way to spend my last night in Atlanta for a while."

She opened her arms, and Mrs. Lucas stepped forward

into her embrace. It was a long hug. I noticed it. When the hug was done, Miss Julia reached out and touched the lock of hair that had come loose from Mrs. Lucas's hairpins. She rubbed the lock between her fingers and thumb, and then tucked it behind Mrs. Lucas's ear. Then she let the tip of her finger move along the skin of Mrs. Lucas's neck, and along the curve between her neck and shoulder, and then all the way across her bare shoulder and down her arm. It was quick. The whole journey of that fingertip took two seconds. But I saw years of intimacy in it.

Miss Julia and Mrs. King left, followed by the bodyguard, disappearing into the cool night, still laughing as they went. When they were gone, and Mrs. Lucas and Mrs. Broussard turned back to the house and saw me, they both looked concerned. "Doris?" Mrs. Lucas said, moving toward me. "Are you alright?"

I wasn't. My heart was racing, and my knees felt shaky. "I . . . need to lie down," I said.

"I'll help you to your room," she said.

I shook my head. "No. I'll be alright on my own."

"Are you sure?"

"Yes, ma'am."

She looked like she was about to argue, but I turned away, walking down the hallway as fast as my wobbly knees would let me, to the back of the house and down the stairs.

6

When I was ten years old, my mother told me that a woman cannot love another woman the same way a man can. She told me this because a woman at our church had recently been possessed by demons who'd warped her mind and made her think she wanted to sleep with other women. The demons had compelled her to write down her unnatural thoughts in a diary. Her husband found this diary and took it to Pastor Mills, desperate for help. As happens, these folks' business got out all around church. The diary, which nobody but the husband and Pastor saw directly, but which was much speculated about, and the de-demoning efforts that followed, were all anybody could talk about for weeks. I'd got wind of it all one morning in church, when I heard some older girls whispering about it in the next pew, and later I asked my mother how they knew it was demons that made this woman feel the way she did, and not just her own sinful proclivities. All humans were born into sin, after all. How could Pastor know the difference between regular sinful thoughts and full-on demon possession?

"Some thoughts is beyond sinful," Ma said.

"Which ones?"

She put down her ironing and looked at me. "Women got roles, Doris. We mothers and wives and sisters. Them roles is the bedrock of family. Of the community. But we can't fill them roles if we off somewhere thinking thoughts only men ought to think. 'Sides, it's a waste of time. A woman can love another woman plenty good ways, but she can't love her the way a man can."

"Why not?"

"Because it aint the way God meant it to be."

That sounded like the answer to a different question, not the one I was asking, but the look on Ma's face told me to let it go. Even though I didn't understand why a woman *couldn't* love another woman that way, I did understand that she *shouldn't.* So, the first thing I did when I got back to my room at Mrs. Broussard's was fetch the Bible out my pillowcase, get down on my knees, and pray for my teacher's soul.

"Dear Lord in heaven, please deliver Mrs. Lucas from the sin of being an invert, which everybody know is one of the worst sins of all. You destroyed Sodom and Gomorrah on account of that particular evil." I squeezed my eyes closed tighter, to give the prayer more power. "Maybe this all my fault, Jesus. I asked Mrs. Lucas to help me, and she brought me here, and I know she mean well, but I don't feel right being in this Godless house. Lord, I know you the architect and master of all things, so if I'm here it must be because you want me to be here. Maybe you wanted me to see what I saw so I can help Mrs. Lucas somehow. Then again, maybe this my punishment for wanting to get rid of this baby. Or it's your way of telling me I need to go home. Shit, I don't know. Sweet Jesus, I'm so confused." Suddenly, I felt a cool breeze on my skin. I took it as a sign that God was listening. I held the Bible tight to my chest. "I'm confused, Lord, but I know you aint never confused. Please help me to see your purpose for bringing me among these heathens. And, Lord, while you at it, please forgive me for the sins I've committed. And for the one I'm still planning to commit tomorrow. Amen."

"Amen," came a voice from behind me.

I dropped the Bible and leapt up from the floor, turned, and saw a young white man standing by the window. I stared at him, unable to move, fear coursing through me.

"No, no, no," he said, holding up his hands as if to block the panic on my face. "It's okay. Don't worry, I'm colored."

Don't worry, I'm colored aint a sentence you hear every day.

"I live here," he said. "This is my uncle's house. This is my room."

That's when I remembered what Mrs. Broussard had said, about her delinquent step-nephew. I peered at him.

Mr. Broussard was high-yellow enough to pass for white if he wanted to. But this boy would've had a hard time *not* passing, even if he wasn't inclined toward it. He had beige skin, greenish-brown eyes, wavy, sandy hair that was cut close on the sides and combed back on top, sort of like a conk but without the telltale naps at the roots. The only things about him that looked colored were his nose and lips, which were broader and fuller than a white man's, but you had to look close to see it.

"I come in through the window whenever Auntie Sylvia

banishes me from the premises," he said, in an up North accent. "I didn't expect anybody to be in here. Certainly nobody as pretty as you. What's your name, sweet thing?"

"It aint 'sweet thing,'" I said. "That's for sho."

He laughed. "I'm Dexter Porter." He offered me his hand.

I ignored it. "How long you been standing there?"

He shrugged. "Not long. I did hear something about committing sins, though. What sins you looking to commit? Maybe I can help." He smiled in a lewd way.

"It aint right to eavesdrop," I said.

"Maybe the Lord will forgive me," he said, "if you sneak in a prayer on my behalf."

I squinted my eyes at him. "It aint right to blaspheme, neither."

"It aint right to be in somebody's room and not even tell that somebody your name."

I looked him over. Besides the fact of looking near-white, and not showing any real reverence unto the Lord, he seemed alright. I'd known a few delinquents in my time, and he didn't come off as one out the gate.

"My name Doris Steele," I told him.

"Doris Steele," he repeated, nodding. "What you doing in my room, Doris Steele?"

"I'm here with my teacher, visiting your auntie."

He made a face like he thought that was strange, and I remembered I was supposed to be Mrs. Lucas's niece.

"I'll never cease to be amazed by how many friends Auntie Sylvia has," he said. "Why do people choose to spend time with her, when they don't have to? It's one of the great mysteries of the universe, as far as I'm concerned." He shrugged. "But it takes all kinds, I guess. That's what they say, anyhow."

I'd never heard anybody say that, but I nodded right on.

"You go to Spelman?" he asked. "I don't remember seeing you at any parties."

"I'm still in high school," I said, even though I'd quit.

"Where?" he asked. "Booker T.?"

"Burgess Landrum."

He shook his head. "Never heard of it."

"It's in Millen," I said, and when he looked blank, I added, "It's a few hours from here."

"Oh, you're visiting from out of town! I'm not from Atlanta, either. I'm from Philadelphia."

"What you doing down here?"

"I go to Morehouse."

"They aint got colleges up North?" I asked.

"Well, my uncle pays for my schooling," he said, "and Morehouse is his alma mater, so . . . here I am." He pulled a small brown paper bag out of his pocket. "You want some reefer?"

What in Holy Jesus's name? "Of course not!" I told him, taking a step back.

"Alright, alright," he said. "I'm only trying to be friendly. Don't have a baby over it."

I started toward the door.

"Where you going?" he called after me.

"To ask your auntie for a different room."

"If you do that, she'll know I'm here!"

That sounded like a Dexter problem, not a Doris problem. But I didn't want to be unkind, so I asked, "Well, where I'm supposed to sleep, then?"

He grinned. "It's a big bed."

I moved for the door again, calling, "Mrs. Brou—!"

"Okay, okay," he said, rushing after me. "Listen. I can crash at my buddy Lonnie's place again. But he works the night shift, and he won't be home for another hour. Just let me stay here until then."

I didn't want him to stay an hour. I had things on my mind, things I needed to sort out. He must've seen the *no* on my face, because he said, "It's the Christian thing to do, isn't it?"

I knew this near-white fool aint give a rat's ass about the Christian thing to do. But he was right. God don't like inhospitableness.

"Fine," I told him. "One hour."

He smiled.

I picked up my Bible and sat down on the edge of a chair. I flipped to Genesis 19:1, the story of Sodom and Gomorrah, and read silently. But I could feel Dexter watching me, and I couldn't concentrate. Finally, he asked, "What you doing?"

"What it look like I'm doing?"

"Reading the Bible."

"Well, then."

He watched me for a few more moments, then laughed. "You sure you don't want some reefer?"

I glared at him over top of the Good Book.

"I'm only kidding," he said. He sat down on the bed, grabbed his bag, and opened it. "I have something else I want to give you."

He held out a sheet of paper. At the top, it read: "The Student Nonviolent Coordinating Committee Conference." And below that there was a schedule.

"You should come to one of the nonviolence workshops," he said. "Tomorrow from nine to eleven."

"I'm busy then."

"Well, there's gonna be stuff going on all day," he said. "Trust me, this aint something a smart girl like yourself wants to miss. Snick is the future of the movement."

"I already got enough to do without adding the civil rights movement to the list. And how you know I'm a smart girl, anyhow?"

"I can tell. Something curious in your eyes." He locked eyes with mine and smiled.

I frowned back at him. He was too high-yellow for my taste, and besides, I was here to get an abortion, not to make eyes at some boy.

"You heard about the sit-ins we've been staging all over this city?"

I looked at the paper again. "You part of the SNCC?"

"We pronounce it *Snick*. And, yeah, I am. Me and a whole lot of other young Negroes who've had enough."

I wondered why Mrs. Broussard hadn't mentioned her own nephew was part of the sit-ins she hated so much.

"We got another round of demonstrations planned for

next week," Dexter said. "Martin Luther King's gonna be with us this time." He put a finger to his lips. "Don't tell anybody, though. That's top secret."

"I guess they shouldn't have told you, then."

"Well, I can tell you're a trustworthy person," he said. "Now, I'm not a follower of King, personally. He trusts these liberal crackers a whole lot more than I do. But I can't deny his presence will bring us the attention we need. The newspapers can't get enough of him."

I stared at him for a moment, at his light skin and greenish eyes. "You ever used a whites-only toilet?" I asked him.

His smile faltered and he stammered. "I—no. I mean . . . of course not. That would be a betrayal of colored people who can't do the same." And he smiled again, looking proud of his answer.

He sounded righteous, but I knew he was lying, and I wondered where he got off criticizing Reverend King while walking around in white skin. I didn't like it one bit. He must've known what I was thinking, because he changed the subject quick as a flicker. "You like Ray Charles?" he asked me.

"Naw."

He frowned. "Who don't like Ray Charles?"

"Why you even ask me, then?" I was messing with him now, Jesus forgive me, but I couldn't help myself.

He walked over to a cabinet, opened it, and fingered through a row of records inside, before pulling one out. He held it up. "You heard his last one?"

"Only the singles," I said. Ma and Daddy didn't allow anything but gospel in our house, so I had to go down to Lena's to listen to the devil's music. Lena had a whole bunch of records—Chubby Checker, Dinah Washington, and plenty of Ray Charles, including "I Got a Woman," "What'd I Say," and "Let the Good Times Roll," all singles we'd listened to over and over.

"There's some good stuff on here that didn't get released as singles," Dexter said. "Let me play one for you." He removed the vinyl from the sleeve and moved to the record player. "This is called, 'Come Rain or Come Shine.'"

I watched him, vexed that he didn't even wait for me to say yes. I couldn't think with him there, and now I couldn't read my Bible, either. I thought again about hollering for Mrs. Broussard, but then the music started, and the sound of melancholy trumpets filled the air, and I reckoned I might just as well listen to the song first. *I'm gonna love you, like no one's loved you,* Ray Charles sang, and I sat back in the chair and felt it wash over me.

I've never been much of a romantic. I wasn't back then, and I'm not now. At seventeen, most of what people called love looked to me like plain old obligation. But I was interested in love songs, because I liked thinking about how the words came together, or bounced off each other, to capture a certain feeling. When Ray sang, *We're in or we're out of the money,* I thought about how people said "in the money" or "out of money," but nobody ever said, "out of *the* money," and I wondered how the person who wrote the song decided to phrase it just so.

"Nice, huh?" Dexter asked when the song had ended.

I nodded.

"That's the last song on the record. You want me to play the whole thing from the beginning?"

"Alright," I said, glad he'd thought to ask this time. And, anyway, what was the harm? Maybe it was better not to think about Mrs. Lucas, to get it off my mind for a spell.

While Dexter was starting the record over, I noticed a book on the bed that had fallen out of his bag, and I picked it up.

"You read Baldwin?" he asked when he saw me looking at it.

"Naw. It any good?" I asked, turning the book over in my hands.

"It's better than good," he said.

"What it about?"

"This poor kid in Harlem, trying to figure out his relationship to the church, and to his family. He's got a crazy religious fanatic for a stepdaddy. A lot of it is really messed up. It's semi-autobiographical."

"What?"

"It's about the writer's own life."

"He from Harlem? The writer?"

"Yeah. But he wrote it when he was living in Paris."

I remembered Mrs. Broussard's doctor friend and realized this was the second time that day I'd heard about a Negro living in France. "It's a lot of Negroes there?"

"In France? There's a whole community of expats."

"Expats?"

"Expatriates. People who were born in this country but got fed up and left. It's mostly writers and artists. Josephine Baker's there. My sister's there, too. In Paris."

"What she doing there?"

"Writing a book."

I tried to picture it. In my mind, I saw a colored girl sitting at a typewriter, her dark fingers tapping away. Outside the window, in the distance, was the Eiffel Tower, same as it always looked in movies. The girl was focused, pink tongue poking out the side of her mouth as she worked. After while, I realized Dexter's sister probably didn't have dark fingers, probably didn't even look colored, and that the girl I was picturing was me. I felt silly, imagining myself there, much as I loved to play with words. I shook the picture away.

"What your sister book about?" I asked.

Dexter shrugged. "I don't know. But I'm going to go stay with her in the summer, so I guess I'll find out then." He pointed at the book I was still holding. "You can keep that if you want. I already read it twice. It's a good story. A whole lot better than the one he wrote about homosexuals."

I stared at him. Blinked. "What?"

"*Giovanni's Room.*" He said it like he was talking about a disgusting place, like a kitchen with bad food, or a bathroom nobody ever cleaned. "It's about these white men, these inverts, living in Paris. I don't know why he wanted to write about that. It's not exactly a respectable subject. I guess everybody's trying to write something new, but I wish he'd chosen a different topic. *And* it's about white people. Why does a Negro write a novel about white people? Plenty of white writers already have that covered. But I guess I should be grateful. It'd be worse to portray Negroes in that abnormal way."

I looked away from him, down at the book in my hands. I felt annoyed at what he was saying. Which didn't make any sense because I'd always thought inverts were abnormal, too. I'd been praying for Mrs. Lucas's soul not half an hour ago. I thought again about what I'd seen, about Mrs. Lucas and Julia Avery in the doorway. I should've felt sick about it, the way Dexter sounded when he talked about *Giovanni's Room,* but I realized I didn't know how I truly felt.

Pastor Mills preached a lot about the sin of homosexuality, but it was always about men. Now Dexter was talking about men, too. Besides the possessed woman at church, I never heard much about women who were that way. One time, a year or so ago, Lena told me about two women she saw in Atlanta, standing in a window hugging on each other in an unnatural way.

"What you think they do together? In the bed?" I asked Lena.

"One of them act like the woman," she said, "and the other one act like the man."

"That don't make no sense," I said.

"It aint supposed to make sense."

Sitting there listening to Ray Charles, thinking about Mrs. Lucas and Julia Avery, I started to wonder again what women did together in bed, but I stopped myself because I reckoned Jesus wouldn't want me pondering such a thing. Instead, I wondered why, if Mrs. Lucas *was* an invert, she'd married a man? Had she always been one, or was it something she'd picked up recently? And what about Mrs. Broussard? Was she one? How could she be, when I'd just met her husband? Besides, I'd always been told that inverts led sordid lives. Mrs. Broussard's life looked peachy. Julia Avery's life looked even peachier than that, far as *Jet* magazine was telling it. I didn't know what to make of any of that. I wanted Dexter to leave, so I could think it all through. But when I looked over, he was asleep. I hurried over to the bed and tried to shake him awake. He just snored and rolled over. *This high-yellow nigga got some damn nerve,* I thought.

"Doris? Is everything alright?" Mrs. Lucas asked when she opened the door and saw me.

"Yes, ma'am. Sorry to wake you."

She was wearing a short chiffon nightgown, her hair hung loose in a tumble against her shoulders, and she was holding a book in one hand. "I wasn't asleep," she said, holding up *The Bean Eaters*. "I've been trying to calm my mind with Gwendolyn Brooks. What's wrong, sugar?"

"It's a quadroon in my room."

She peered at me. "What?"

"Or maybe a octoroon," I said. "Mrs. Broussard nephew. He snuck in through the window."

"My word." She looked concerned. "Well, that won't do at all, will it?"

"Can I sleep in here?" I asked her. "I don't mind the floor."

"There's a couch. And of course you can," she said, and stepped aside to let me in.

This room was even bigger than Dexter's, decorated in

warm browns and violets, with a king-sized bed that had an intricately carved headboard. There was a dresser and a Murphy desk and, over by the window, a couch, which was the same violet color as the heavy curtains that hung at the large windows. They were thrown open, the cool night air filling the room with the green smells of trees.

"This place sure is nice," I said, taking it all in.

"Good taste and a pile of money go a long way." She nodded toward the nightclothes I was carrying and said, "The bathroom's here," and led me over to the door, opened it, and switched on the light. "I'll look for some extra sheets and blankets. Let me know if you need anything, sugar."

"Yes, ma'am. Thank you." I went on inside the bathroom and shut the door.

Unlike my yellow and aqua bathroom down the hall, everything in this bathroom was bright pink, from the sink and counter to the commode and bathtub, to the tile on the walls and the floor. I placed my nightclothes on the shiny pink counter and noticed Mrs. Lucas had set up her beauty products in a perfect straight line below the mirror. I ran my fingers over eyeliner, mascara, and three different tubes of lipstick. I picked up a small jar of Pond's, twisted off the top, and sniffed the thick white cold cream inside. Gardenias. Then I pulled the top off a small bottle of perfume that smelled like Mrs. Lucas, sandalwood with a hint of orange peels.

The moment replayed in my head again. Julia Avery slipping her arm around Mrs. Lucas's waist. Julia Avery running her finger down Mrs. Lucas's arm. Standing in the bathroom now, I wasn't at all sure anymore about what it meant. At the time, it had seemed so clear, so intimate, so scandalous. But now I wondered how I could've been sure. These women were so different, in so many ways, from me and from other women I knew. Maybe that was just the way rich Negroes behaved. And besides, Mrs. Lucas hadn't actually done anything. It was Julia Avery who put her arms around her. Mrs. Lucas had moved away. It was Julia Avery who touched her neck and shoulders. Maybe Mrs. Lucas hadn't liked it. Or maybe that's just the way Miss Julia was sometimes. They were old friends, after all.

I put down the perfume and looked at myself in the mirror over the sink. There were bags under my eyes. I looked like I hadn't slept since Jesus was in kindergarten.

I undressed and put on my nightgown. Then I folded my clothes, sat them on a chair next to the bathroom door, and went back into the bedroom.

Mrs. Lucas had made up the couch with some sheets and a blanket. She was reclining there, reading her book. I looked from her to the bed.

"You need a good night's sleep tonight more than I do," she said.

"I feel bad putting you out your own bed," I said.

She waved a hand. "It's not my bed, anyway. It's fine, sugar. I'll be fine right here." She closed her book. "Let's get some sleep."

I hesitated, but I reckon I was too tired to protest any more than I already had. So, I climbed into the bed, turned out the side lamp, and settled myself under the covers, noticing the faint smell of gardenias on the pillows.

As I lay there falling asleep, I decided, whatever I'd seen or hadn't seen, whatever it meant or didn't, Mrs. Lucas was the person I trusted most in the world. Still. Even if she might be a hell-bound sinner.

7

hen I woke up the next morning, the clock on the desk said seven twenty-five. Mrs. Lucas was already gone, and the sheets from the couch were folded neatly on top of the dresser. I made the bed, then went into the bathroom and grabbed yesterday's clothes, and left the room.

In the hallway, I could smell food cooking, and I could hear the faint sound of voices coming from upstairs. I went down the hall to Dexter's room and saw he was gone. He'd left *Go Tell It on the Mountain* at the foot of the bed.

I showered, brushed my teeth and combed my hair, then got dressed. There was a loose thread on the sleeve of my blouse. I wrapped it around my finger and tried to break it, but I couldn't, so I tucked it up under and went upstairs.

In the upstairs hallway, the smell of food was so strong it made me feel sick. I had to run back downstairs to throw up. I hadn't eaten anything, so it was just bitter yellow acid in the bowl.

When I finally made it to the kitchen, I found a different

maid there. Instead of Pearl, there was a younger woman, probably not much older than me. I stood at the door and watched her for a few moments while she flipped hotcakes on a large skillet. Then I made myself known. "Morning, ma'am."

She looked up at me, surprised, and I thought maybe she wasn't used to being called ma'am at work. "Morning," she said. "You must be Doris."

I nodded.

"I'm Sharon. Nice to meet you."

"What happened to Pearl?"

"Oh, she don't come in until eleven. I'm the morning help," she said. "If you looking for your auntie, she out on the porch with Mrs. Broussard. You want coffee?"

"No, thank you, ma'am."

She giggled. "Alright. Well, let me know if you change your mind." She went back to flipping hotcakes.

I followed the sounds of voices to the front of the house and out onto the porch, where I found Mrs. Lucas sitting on the porch swing, and Mrs. Broussard leaning against the railing. Both of them were drinking coffee, and they were laughing about something.

"Doris!" Mrs. Broussard said when she saw me. "We were just talking about you."

"You were?" I asked, feeling self-conscious all of a sudden.

"I was telling Sylvia about your visitor last night," Mrs. Lucas said.

"You must've been appalled," said Mrs. Broussard, but she sounded like she thought it was funny. "I know I always am, whenever I spend time with Dexter."

"He wasn't so bad," I told her.

She made a face like she didn't believe me. "Well, I promise you it won't happen again."

I nodded and mumbled a thank you, but I felt guilty, like I'd tattled on the boy and got him in trouble.

"You want some coffee, hun? I can have Sharon bring some out to you."

"No, thank you, ma'am. I don't think I could keep it down."

"Come sit," Mrs. Lucas said, patting the seat next to her.

I sat down beside her on the swing. She'd done her hair different this morning. It wasn't pinned up anymore. It fell against her shoulders, curled under at the ends. And she was barefoot again.

Sharon appeared in the doorway, wiping her hands on a kitchen rag. "Phone call, Mrs. Broussard."

Mrs. Broussard excused herself and went inside.

"How you feeling, Doris?" Mrs. Lucas asked me when we were alone. "Still having morning sickness?"

"Yes, ma'am. And my stomach in knots besides. I'm ready to get this all over with. When can we go?"

"We'll leave in about an hour," she said. "Try to relax until then." She put her arm around my shoulders, and the light scent of sandalwood and citrus on her skin made me feel a little better, a little calmer, the way I felt when I was small and I sat in Ma's lap, and her smell, of lavender and rose and sweat, wrapped around me. We sat there like that, gently swinging, saying nothing, while a morning breeze rustled the leaves of the trees and the potted plants on the porch.

After a couple of minutes, Mrs. Broussard came out of the

house with a worried look on her face. "That was the doctor," she told us. "There's a delay."

I shot up off the swing. "What kind of delay?"

"Settle down now," Mrs. Broussard said. "He won't be able to make ten o'clock, is all."

Is all?

My stomach twisted on itself. "What time, then?"

"He doesn't know yet. He says to sit tight and he'll call us soon."

"Soon?" Mrs. Lucas asked, standing up, too. "Soon, as in an hour? Soon, as in a day?"

"A couple of hours, maybe."

"*Maybe?* What did the man *say,* Syl?"

"He said before lunchtime, hopefully."

"*Hopefully?*" Now she sounded irritated. "That's not very reassuring, Sylvia."

Mrs. Broussard threw her hands up. "Well, what do you want me to do, Catie? Call his office to complain? It's an *abortion,*" she said, whispering that single word, "not a hernia, y'all. It's a delicate situation."

Mrs. Lucas sighed.

"I'm sure he'll call us before lunchtime," Mrs. Broussard said, looking at me, "and you'll have the whole thing done with in time for *As the World Turns.*"

She was making it sound like a sure thing, but my mind was spinning with the *maybe*s and *hopefully*s of a few seconds ago. What if he didn't call? What if he called to say he couldn't do it anymore? Then what? I wanted to scream at her: As the World Turns *don't even play on Saturdays!*

"Well, we'll just have to wait, then," said Mrs. Lucas. "There's nothing else for it."

But the idea of waiting, even for a few hours, felt to me like looking out across the ocean for land that was nowhere in sight.

I was too anxious to eat breakfast, so I went back to my room and paced for a long time, so long I got myself overheated and had to open a window. Finally, I lay down on the bed, closed my eyes, and prayed to Jesus for help. *I know you don't approve of what I'm doing, Lord. But I pray for your mercy, anyhow. I can't have a baby. Not now, Lord. Not yet. I aint ready. And I don't know how to get ready. I don't know how to make myself want this.*

"Hey, Doris Steele."

I jumped up. Dexter was at the open window, grinning in at me.

"You can't come in!" I said, moving to shut it.

He grabbed the window from underneath to stop me from closing it. "You willing to break my fingers to keep me out?"

"If your fingers get broke, it's your own damn fault!"

"Ooh, language, church girl," he said, and grinned again. "What will Jesus say?"

I pushed down harder on the window.

"Okay, okay, listen. I left my wallet here," he said. "I only came back to get it."

"I don't believe you!"

"I swear. I thought you'd be out. That's what you told me, remember?"

I had told him that. "Fine," I said, letting go of the window. "Wait right there and I'll bring it to you. Where you leave it?"

"On the dresser," he said.

I went over to the dresser and saw the wallet. I picked it up. "Here," I said, shoving it at him. "Now you can git."

"Why so hostile?" he asked, putting the wallet in his back pocket. "I thought we were friends, Doris Steele."

"We aint. Friends don't take your bed without asking and push you out your room."

"*Whose* bed?" he asked. "*Whose* room?"

He had a point, but I was on a roll now. "If it hadn't been for Mrs.—uh—my auntie Cate letting me have *her* bed, I don't know what I woulda done."

"You might have had to sleep in Olivia's room. Or the boys' room. Or the other guest room," he said, shaking his head in mock pity. "Poor thing."

"Why aint *you* sleep in one of them rooms, then?"

"Because *this* is my room. Which Sylvia had no right to throw me out of."

"Well, that's between you and her," I said, and started to close the window again, right down on his fingers.

"You lied," he said. "I thought lying was a sin against the Lord."

I stopped, peering at him. "What you talking about, lied?"

"When you told me you had plans this morning."

"I did. They just got moved to later on." My stomach churned again.

Dexter peered at me. "You okay?"

"What?"

"You seem anxious."

I shook my head. "I'm fine. I just hate waiting. I aint never been no good at it."

"Well, why don't you come down to the conference with me?" he asked. "It'll take your mind off waiting, at least."

I opened my mouth to say no, but then I thought, *Well, why not?* It beat sitting around here watching the clock. Besides, I was growing more curious about the sit-ins. I wanted to hear what the students in Atlanta were up to.

"Alright," I said.

Dexter looked surprised, maybe because I'd threatened to smash his fingers in the window not thirty seconds before. "Okay, cool," he said. "Meet me upstairs." And he walked off, away from the window and around the house, out of sight.

I went into the bathroom to relieve myself, and while I was sitting there, I heard the doorbell ring. I hurried up and flushed, grabbed a sweater on my way out the room, and went upstairs.

Dexter was in the living room with Mrs. Broussard and Mrs. Lucas.

"I was considering Cheyney," he was saying to Mrs. Lucas when I came in, "but I'm glad I listened to Uncle Alonzo and chose Morehouse. I'm getting a whole different kind of education than I would have gotten up North." When he saw me standing there, he said, "Oh, hello. Who's this fine young lady?"

"This is Doris," Mrs. Broussard said. "Catie's niece."

Dexter took a step toward me. "Nice to meet you, Doris," he said, extending his hand to me.

Mrs. Broussard reached out and slapped it away.

"Ow! Jesus, Aunt Syl!"

"We know you snuck into Doris's room last night," Mrs. Broussard said. "So, you can drop the act, Sidney Poitier."

Dexter gave me a pained look. "You told her?"

"I aint mean to."

"And here I was thinking we were soulmates."

Mrs. Broussard looked at Mrs. Lucas with raised eyebrows. "Mmm-hmm. Boys lining up. What'd I tell you?" She looked at Dexter, who was still rubbing the back of his hand. "Why are you in my house, boy? I thought I made it clear you're no longer welcome here."

"I know you don't mean it, Aunt Syl," he said, smiling.

Mrs. Broussard didn't smile back.

"Fine," he said. "I'm only here to get Doris. I'm taking her to the conference."

"What conference?" Mrs. Lucas asked.

"He's one of those student activists doing the sit-ins," Mrs. Broussard explained.

"We do more than sit-ins. Our national conference is this weekend." He fished out the schedule from his bag and handed it to Mrs. Lucas.

"Can I go?" I asked her. "Just for an hour or so? I think I'll lose my sanity if I have to sit around and wait for the . . ." I glanced at Dexter, then back at her. "If I have to sit around and wait."

"How far is it?" Mrs. Lucas wanted to know.

"Not far at all, ma'am," Dexter replied. "Just down by the colleges."

Mrs. Lucas checked her watch. "Can you have her back here before noon?"

"Yes, ma'am."

Mrs. Broussard frowned. "Catie. You can't leave this child in the care of a juvenile delinquent."

Dexter bristled. "That's not fair, Aunt Syl. I'm a college-educated man, an upstanding citizen."

"You're not college-educated yet," she said. "If I'd had my way, Alonzo would've cut off your tuition ten times by now. And I don't even know what to say to you calling yourself an upstanding citizen, while you steal from your own family."

"I never stole anything except to give it away to someone who needed it more," he said. "Besides, I never even saw you wear any of that jewelry."

"Catie, trust me when I say you don't want this hoodlum sniffing around this child."

It was the second time she'd called me a child in the span of a minute, and I was on the verge of taking offense. "I'll be alright, Mrs. Broussard," I said. "I can handle boys."

She looked at me, then at my belly, and said, "You sure, hun?"

8

Dexter drove a 1954 Pontiac Chieftain, dark green inside and out. "My parents bought it," he told me. "They don't have too much money, but my father doesn't like Uncle Alonzo buying me everything. He thinks Uncle tries to show him up."

"Does he?"

"Maybe. My mother is Uncle's only sister. They were real close growing up. Uncle wanted her to marry somebody from Atlanta and stay close by. But she married my father and moved with him to Philadelphia. Uncle could never hate her, so I guess he hates my father instead. They got some kind of macho pissing contest going on for the last twenty years."

"What you mean when you said you stole from your family to give it away to people who need it?" I asked him.

"Just that. I hocked some jewelry my aunt and uncle never wear and gave the money to the cause."

"What cause?"

"Snick. This conference, to be exact."

"How come you aint just ask your uncle for the money?

Maybe he woulda give it to you. You said he buy you everything."

"I did ask. And they made a respectable donation. They always do."

"But you still stole from them? Why?"

"I told you. They *never* wore that jewelry. Which means, not only did they not need it, they didn't even really want it."

"If they didn't want it, why they kick you out the house for stealing it?"

"They didn't. *Sylvia* did," he said. "Look, my aunt and uncle and I have some agreements. *Unspoken* agreements, you know what I mean? They pay for my college in the hopes that I'll one day become a lawyer or a doctor, make a fortune that'll guarantee the continued esteem—nay, *reverence*—of the Broussard family, and I, in turn, stay out of their business. Auntie Sylvia's not mad about that jewelry, she's mad I was plundering around in her things."

"Mad enough to throw you out? For some 'plundering around'?"

"She's like that," he said. "Secretive. One time, I saw her reading a letter and I asked who it was from. You would've thought I asked what color underwear she had on, the way she cut her eyes at me."

"Some folks don't like everybody in they business," I said, surprised to find myself defending Mrs. Broussard. I wasn't sure I liked her any more than her step-nephew did. But one thing I knew about her was that she was generous. She said she gave to the NAACP. And Dexter just admitted she gave to SNCC, even though she didn't approve of them. And she was paying for my abortion, if I ever got one. I wondered what *this* Negro ever gave anybody. I started to feel real annoyed with him again, and then I remembered the book he'd given me last night, and the distraction he was giving me now, and I softened toward him again.

From Collier Heights, we drove toward downtown Atlanta. I could see the city skyline, and I was amazed at how tall the buildings were, some of them stretching twenty stories or more into the sky. This was by far the biggest city I'd ever been in, and I poked my head out the window and stared out at it, not caring if I came off like a rube. Closer to downtown, I saw huge billboards for Coca-Cola and Ford Motors, and, way up ahead, something that looked like a cross between a trolley and a bus. When I asked Dexter which one it was, he said it was a trolleybus, but that they called them "trackless trolleys" in Atlanta. We passed a sprawling park, and I saw colored families picnicking in the shade of oak trees, kids and teenagers riding bicycles, running in the grass, and throwing balls around. "This is Washington Park," Dexter told me. "It was the first park for colored people in Atlanta."

On the car radio, a song ended and another began, filling the car with Julia Avery's voice. The song was called "Got to Have That Man," and she sure sang it like she meant it.

I glanced over at Dexter's profile as he drove. Light-skinned as he was, he wasn't bad looking. His eyes were pretty. And he had those lips. I wondered what he kissed like. A colored boy or a white boy? Was there a difference? Maybe I ought to kiss him and find out. *Lord Jesus, forgive me for my sinful thoughts.* But then I remembered what Mrs. Lucas said about the cosmos. And I thought maybe Jesus didn't care if I thought about kissing this boy or not. Maybe Jesus wasn't studying me at all. But right at that moment, we pulled into the parking lot of a church. "Here we are," Dexter said, turning off the car. I looked up at the steeple and I thought, *Well, shit.*

No matter what was going on in my life, being inside a church almost always made me feel better. Church had been part of my life from my very beginning. It was the most constant, unchanging thing I knew. Every church I'd ever been in was different, but the same, too, and there was a comfort in that sameness, especially when everything outside those walls felt so unfamiliar. As we passed a large sanctuary, the pews, the position of the pulpit, even the dust that danced in the light through the windows, made me feel steadier. The smells of old wood and the church ladies' perfume that had leaked into it over years made the world, so strange in the last twenty-four hours, feel known again. I saw a group of people, twenty-five of them, maybe, sitting in one section of pews, listening to a man who was standing in front of them, reading off a piece of paper. I couldn't hear him clear enough to know what he was saying, but the folks listening to him sure looked interested. I followed Dexter down a short flight of stairs, to the basement. There was a large, open room with an empty baptismal pool in it, a piano in the corner, and a few smaller rooms off the main one. I followed Dexter to a door with a handwritten sign tacked up on it. GORDON CAREY. CONGRESS OF RACIAL EQUALITY. NON-

VIOLENCE WORKSHOP 6. Dexter moved to push the door open, but I grabbed his arm.

"Hold on, now," I said. "I thought we come to hear a speech."

"A speech?" He scoffed. "Snick is about action, Doris Steele, not a whole bunch of words that don't make any difference in the end. This is activism, not *talkivism.*" He pushed the door open. Then, seeing the frown still on my face, he whispered, "Nobody's going to force you to participate. You can just sit in the back and watch. As long as you don't mind looking like a Fed." He grinned and went through the door.

I hesitated. Behind me, a stout boy with round glasses said, "Excuse me, miss," and I stepped out the way and let him pass. I saw two young women walking down the hallway, the way Dexter and me had come. They walked quick, like they had somewhere important to be. I don't know why, but I followed them.

I kept a few feet back as they walked to the end of the hallway, around a corner, and through a door. I followed and found myself in a bathroom. Which wasn't what I'd expected. I must've looked surprised, because one of them, who was examining her face in the mirror over the sink, said, "You lost, dear? You looking for one of the workshops?"

I didn't want to tell them I'd followed them in there, so I said, "No, I just need to wash my hands," and turned on one of the taps.

"I'm just tired of all the lip service gets paid to having female leadership. But then they always talk before us, and over us, every chance they get. We did all the work organizing this conference, months of planning, until here come the men, swooping in to lead the workshops and grab the glory."

"It's not about the glory, Ruby."

"I know. But really, Diane. *Seventeen* workshops, and only *two* run by women. And they're both at the same time! It's disgraceful. I bet you don't get half the attendees the men get."

"Thanks for the vote of confidence," Diane said.

Ruby shook her head, frustrated. "It's not a reflection of you, or the important work you're doing. That's my point. It's plain old male chauvinism."

"Your hands must be very dirty," Diane said, and when I looked up, she was watching me. "What you been doing to get such dirty hands?"

"Oh," I replied, and couldn't think of anything else.

"What's your name, little sister?" Ruby asked.

"Doris," I told her, turning off the tap.

"Same as me," she said, pleased. "I'm Ruby Doris. This here's Diane. Where you go?"

"Go?"

"To college," they said at the same time.

"I'm still in high school," I told them. "But I aint from here."

"Where you from?"

"Millen."

"Where the hell is that?" Ruby asked.

"Ruby! My goodness!" Then, looking at me, Diane said, "I keep telling her everybody aint from Atlanta."

"I can't keep track of all the Podunk towns in Georgia," Ruby replied, with a little laugh.

"Most of Georgia Podunk towns," I said.

"Exactly." She smiled. "So, what's the movement like in Milling?"

"Millen. There aint one."

"You ought to start one, then," Ruby said.

"Oh, I aint . . ." I stammered. "I mean, I'm just here visiting. A friend brought me by to kill some time."

They gave each other a look.

"I aint mean it that way," I said. "I'm curious 'bout what y'all doing. I just . . . I aint a activist."

"Who's an activist?" Diane asked. "Nobody. Until they are one."

"What workshops you planning on checking out?" Ruby asked me. "To kill time at?"

"My friend's in Nonviolence Workshop Six."

"You see?" she asked, looking at Diane. "Run by a man. And a white man, no less."

Diane nodded. "Sure. But Gordon's a good guy."

"Diane here's running a workshop on jail versus bail," Ruby told me. "Seven o'clock, upstairs. Come, alright? Bring your friend. More friends if you got 'em."

I nodded, knowing good and damn well I wouldn't be nowhere near here at seven o'clock. God willing, I'd be recovering, resting up for my return home tomorrow.

• • •

When I got back to the door marked Nonviolence Workshop 6, I pushed it open as quiet as I could, and stepped into a room that looked like it was used for Sunday school when it wasn't being used for activism. The walls were painted bright yellow, and there was a big stack of children's picture Bibles on top of a cabinet. Child-sized chairs were pushed against a wall on one side of the room, to make space for twenty or so adult-sized chairs, about half of which were set up in two rows off to the other side of the room. Almost all the seats were taken, filled by people who didn't look much older than I was. It surprised me how many of them were white—a quarter, probably—sitting there side by side with the colored people.

Some stools were lined up in a row in the center of the room, facing the others. Ten young Negroes, men and women both, sat in them. They were staring straight ahead, over the heads of the onlookers, but at nothing in particular besides the wall. Behind them a tall white man walked up and down the row, to the end and back again. The room was quiet except for the sound of his shoes clacking on the wood floor. I reckoned this was the man whose name was on the door, Gordon Carey.

I saw Dexter sitting in the front row of chairs off to the side. I went and sat down in the row behind him and tapped him on the shoulder.

"Where you been?" he whispered.

"Bathroom," I whispered back.

"All this time? You sick?"

I shook my head, no.

"That's fine, very good," the tall white man said to the young people who were staring into nothing. "Now just continue to concentrate on your own imaginary point on the wall, try not to make eye contact with any person, and remember to breathe."

"Where all these white people come from?" I whispered to Dexter. I'd never sat in a room with this many white folks and it didn't feel right. "Georgia?"

He made a face and shook his head. "Hell, no. Mostly from up North. Michigan, New Hampshire, New York."

Mmm-hmm. That's what I thought. Southern whites loved segregation like hogs loved shit.

"The sit-ins that have taken place in Atlanta so far have been largely peaceful," the tall white man said. "White Atlantans like to give the outside world the impression they're too civilized, too cultured, and too busy for violence. It's better for tourism and attracting business from Northern states. The Klan's more likely to show up later, do a big rally after you're gone, to remind everyone that they're always close by. That said, you can never go into it expecting everything will go alright. You must be prepared for anything. Now, Carl and Dexter here are going to act as your antagonists." He gestured to Dexter and a young man sitting beside him, and they got up and walked toward the row of people. "No matter what these men say or do," Carey continued, "I want you to keep looking straight ahead. Don't make eye contact with them and don't react in any way." I could feel the room tense up when he said that. People gave each other nervous glances. The young folks sitting in the center row of stools looked like they were steeling themselves for something. I watched, feeling nervous now myself. The tall white man stepped aside.

Carl and Dexter walked up and down the row of stools,

back and forth. Dexter stopped behind a young man who reminded me of my brother Bud. He had the same wide eyes and the same dimple in his chin. Dexter just stood there behind him, looking like trouble.

Carl walked past Dexter and the boy, to the end of the row and back again. He reached into his pocket and pulled out a pack of cigarettes. He lit one and took a big drag off it. Then he walked right up to a young woman sitting at the end of the row and blew the smoke in her face. She squinted, blinked a few times, and kept on looking ahead.

When I glanced back over at Dexter, he was whispering something to the boy with the dimpled chin. I saw the boy's wide eyes get wider, and then move from his imaginary target on the wall, right to Dexter's face.

"Dexter, look out!" I hollered, on account of this not being the first time I'd seen such a look in a Negro's eyes.

Dexter took a step back, quick, but not quick enough. Before you could say "racial segregation," the boy's fist flew at him. He couldn't get out of reach. The punch landed right in the middle of his face.

"Shit!" Dexter yelled, falling backward.

The boy lunged toward him, but Carl and Gordon both grabbed him and held him back.

Dexter was on the floor, blood running down his face from his nose.

"What the hell is wrong with you?" he yelled at the boy. "I'm colored!"

"You aint colored *enough* to say something like that to me!" He lunged at Dexter again, but Carl had a good grip on him.

Another boy helped Dexter up off the floor. Gordon handed him a handkerchief for his bloody nose, and he came and sat back down. He didn't look at me.

Another young man, a tall, skinny one named Melvin, took Dexter's place. While Carl blew smoke up somebody else's nose, Melvin got in somebody's face, so close their foreheads almost touched. The young woman he was trying to rattle kept her cool, but I saw her hands shaking. I thought about what Mrs. Broussard had said and decided she had a point: Why did we want to eat lunch next to people who hated us so much? It didn't really make sense. But, still, I felt proud of the girl, of all of these folks, seeing what was wrong with the world and trying to do something about it.

Fifteen more minutes passed that way, and then Gordon Carey nodded to Carl and Melvin, and they sat back down. The young protesters all looked relieved to have made it through, even if it was just practice.

"What you say to that boy?" I asked Dexter. We were on our way out the church, headed back to his car. His nose had stopped bleeding but his pride wasn't patched up yet.

"I don't remember," he said.

"You don't remember?" I didn't believe that for a second.

"Not exactly." He shrugged. "I might've called him a baboon. Or a gorilla? I was trying to call him names a white boy would call him. That's the whole point of the exercise."

Ooh chile. "I understand now why he popped you."

He frowned. "I didn't mean anything by it! If he's at a

lunch counter and some ruffians show up, they could do a lot worse than name-calling. What's he going to do then? Punch some white boy in the face and get thrown in jail, or worse?"

I could see his point. But I still couldn't blame the boy. I'd been called monkey by white boys, so I knew how it felt. I wondered if Dexter ever had been. I doubted it.

When we got to his car, he said, "I need to make a stop. Is that okay? It's only eleven. I'll still get you back by noon."

"Stop where?" I asked.

"Just a few blocks from here. I need to drop something off to a friend of mine."

Dexter shook his head. "But I appreciated having it just in case."

"I thought Snick was nonviolent," I said.

The man who'd let us in through the front door laughed. "We look like them Snick kids to you, sweetheart?"

"Lay off, Brother Maurice," Charlie said, putting the pistol down on the table. "Who this young lady we aint had the pleasure of being introduced to?"

"This is Doris," Dexter said. "Doris, this is Charlie Johnson. That's Brother Maurice X. And the bad harmonica player is Erik."

Erik laughed, good-natured, and nodded his head at me. "Pleasure to meet you, Miss Doris."

"She yourn?" Brother Maurice asked Dexter, like I was a baby, or a dog.

"I aint nobody's," I said.

He smiled, and I saw he'd took it to mean I was available.

"Stop looking at the girl like that, Maurice," said the harmonica player. "She aint a side of greens."

"*Brother* Maurice," the man said. "And mind your business, Erik."

"Alright, alright," Charlie said. "Aint no need for all that." He looked from me to Dexter. "Y'all want some sweet tea?"

We sat out on the porch drinking sweet tea, and I listened to the story of how Dexter came to be in need of Charlie's gun.

"Whenever Auntie Sylvia kicks me out, I stay at my friend Lonnie's, just a few doors down from here. Lonnie's part of

Snick, too. So, a few months ago, during the first round of sit-ins, Lonnie got arrested. Now, whenever they arrest us, they put our addresses in the paper."

"It aint to send Christmas cards, neither," Erik said.

"The next day, Charlie here saw four crackers waiting in a car out in the parking lot."

"I figured they was waiting on Lonnie," Charlie said.

"But it so happens, Lonnie was in Cleveland."

"Lucky Lonnie," I said.

"You aint lying," said Charlie. "I told some other fellas I know in the building—vets like me, who got they own guns—and we all agreed to keep a eye out. Couple nights later, them crackers came back. Me and my guys was on they car from four different directions 'fore they knew what was what. I say, 'What y'all doing here?' 'Oh, we waiting on somebody.' I clicked my shotgun and told them to wait somewhere else. They hightailed they asses out of here and aint been back."

"But since I'm crashing at Lonnie's right now," Dexter said, "I wanted to protect myself, just in case. That's why I had the gun. But you know how it is with Snick," he said to Charlie. "Julian threatened to ban me if I didn't give it back."

"Julian who?" I asked.

"Snick's communications director. And one of our founders."

"How he know you had a gun?" I asked.

"That's a real good question," said Erik, holding back a smile.

Dexter frowned.

"I told you not to show it off," Charlie said.

"I didn't show it off!" he insisted. "I only told Lonnie about it. He probably said something to Julian."

"I already told you, you don't need a gun, no way." Charlie sounded offended. "Me, Erik, all of us, we been looking out for you. And Lonnie. And anybody else need looking out for."

"Like bodyguards?" I asked, remembering the one who'd stood outside while Mrs. King was over to Mrs. Broussard's house.

Charlie nodded. "That's right."

"Snick is for nonviolence as a tactic," Dexter told me. "But most of us don't accept it as a way of life."

"And the Klan don't accept it at all," Brother Maurice said. "What you think keeping them from beating them kids down? Or worse? The principles of nonviolent resistance?" He sucked his teeth. "Us. That's what."

"And we aint the only ones, neither," said Charlie. "They got men in Nashville doing the same. Miss'ssippi, too. If it's kids doing nonviolent protests anywhere in the South, it's a bunch of guys like us standing off to the side, making sure they safe, whether they know it or not. You can turn all the cheeks you want. But don't make no mistake, little lady: If you aint got nobody looking out for you, gun loaded and ready to blow a cracker's brains out if need be, this nonviolent shit will get you killed."

"Brother, you aint never lied," Erik said.

"You a bodyguard, too?" I asked him.

"Yes, ma'am." He didn't sound puffed up about it. But I could hear in his voice he took it serious.

"You don't look old enough to be a war vet," I told him.

"I aint. But I learnt how to shoot when I was a kid. Me and Charlie, our daddy learnt us. We growed up in the country, hunting for our food. Where we come from, every Negro got a gun and know how to use it. Wouldn't eat otherwise."

Millen was like that, too, outside of town, where I grew up. Daddy taught me to shoot deer and rabbits when I was about eight.

"But city folks . . . different," Erik said.

"Yeah, that's one word for it," Charlie said.

Erik shook his head. "Some of these college kids, 'specially the ones from up North . . . shit . . . I don't think they know what the Klan capable of."

"You ever shoot one?" I asked him.

He laughed. "Naw. Most times, they see guns, they get out of Dodge quick. They evil but they aint stupid. Most of them, anyhow. They willing to kill to keep us down, sho'nuff. But most of them aint willing to *die* to keep us down."

"You aint scared?" I asked him.

"Sometime," he said, then he smiled a little smile like he was ashamed to say so.

But I thought he was brave. And so handsome, too. My eyes lingered around the hairs peeking out from his unbuttoned shirt. I wondered if they were soft to the touch, or rough. *Jesus, forgive me for my sinful desires. It aint my fault this man so fine. You made him, Lord.*

"Doris." It was Dexter, standing there looking bothered. "I need to get you back."

• • •

In the car, Dexter said, "Don't tell me you're sweet on Erik."

"I aint sweet on nobody," I lied. "But so what if I was? What wrong with him?"

"I heard he got a girl pregnant back in Mississippi and left her there."

I touched my stomach, not thinking. But Dexter didn't see. "Who you hear that from?"

He shrugged. "Just around. It aint hard to believe, though, considering how women act when they get near him."

"How they act?"

"Like they're ready to sacrifice their virtue, that's how. And he aint even that good-looking."

"Say who? You?"

He frowned hard at me. "Tell the truth, now. You think that guy's better looking than m—"

"Yes."

"Damn! You aint want to think about it for a second?"

I laughed. I couldn't help it.

"That's cold-blooded, Doris Steele."

"How come you aint on guard duty?" I asked.

"I'm not scared, if that's what you think."

"Aint nobody said that. I only asked."

He shrugged. "I got a whole lot of respect for Charlie and those guys. But the student movement is nonviolent for a reason."

"What the reason?"

"It works."

"How you know that?" I asked. "Lunch counters still segregated, aint they?"

"For now," Dexter replied. "But Gandhi already showed us what nonviolent resistance can accomplish."

"Who?"

"Gandhi. He was one of the most successful nonviolent activists in history."

I didn't know anything about Gandhi. But, even though I hadn't been in school in a while, I seemed to recall a few times in history where violence got the job done, too.

"If we respond to their unjust laws with violence," Dexter continued, "they say, 'See there? See those niggers acting like animals again? This is why we can't let them have what they want. They're not fit to eat here.' And the whole world believes it. But if we respond with nonviolence, with civil disobedience, they can't paint us that way. And then the world asks what reason they have to keep us out."

Something about his thinking didn't sit right with me, but I wasn't sure what. I thought about Millen, about the race riots, and the fear sent down through generations. "White folks the ones violent," I said. "They start it. They always start it."

"Of course they do. White people are allowed to use as much violence as they want against us, even against each other, as long as they write a good enough story about it. But colored people can't get away with that. Anybody else in the world who meets violence with violence is defending themselves. If we do it, *we're* the violent ones."

"That don't make you mad?"

"Of course it does! We don't choose nonviolence because we're not angry. Or because we're weak or too scared to shoot somebody. We choose it because we think we can win with it."

When we pulled up outside Mrs. Broussard's, he handed me a piece of paper with a phone number on it. "Call me if you want to come back to the conference. Or if you need something else."

"Something else like what?" I asked.

"Reefer. Kisses. Anything," he said, and leaned in my direction.

I thought about letting him kiss me. But I could feel the eye of Jesus upon me, and it's hard to stay horny when the Father, the Son, and the Holy Ghost is all watching, so I scrambled on out the car.

10

rs. Broussard was in the drawing room, alone besides a half-empty glass of booze.

"Afternoon, ma'am," I greeted her.

"Doris," she said. "I'm glad to see you back in one piece."

"Is my auntie here? I mean, Mrs. Lucas?" I could hardly keep the lie straight.

"Catie went to visit her folks," she said, "and then pick up the flowers for the party. Pearl and I are busy with preparations, so she volunteered to go by the florist on her way back."

She didn't look busy. Maybe sitting up straight counted as "busy" to rich Negroes. Then again, she wasn't sitting up all that straight, either.

"I think she probably just wanted to get away from me. She ought to be back any minute. If she's coming back at all."

I shifted my weight, nervous, from one hip to the other.

"Herman hasn't called yet, by the way. The doctor. I'm sure he will soon."

I wanted to go to my room and wait for Mrs. Lucas to get

back. But I felt it would be rude to leave, that Mrs. Broussard would think I didn't want to be around her. 'Course, I didn't. But I was raised better than to let her know that.

"Is there something I can do to help with the party?" I asked.

She took a sip of her drink, then shook her head and said, "No. But come on in and sit by me."

I hesitated.

Mrs. Broussard laughed. "I'm not gonna bite you, hun."

I sat down in a chair.

"You want a drink? Pearl can bring you a Coke. Or something stronger?" She nodded toward the liquor cabinet.

"Oh, no, ma'am! I don't drink. Liquor is the devil's tool." It was rude, considering she was at that very moment having herself a healthy dose, but I'd said it without thinking.

She didn't look offended, though, just interested. "Tool for what?"

"Leading us astray from God's path," I told her.

"What path do you imagine God wants me on right now that this rum is leading me astray from?"

I could imagine any number of holy-minded things a person might get done if they weren't already liquored up at a quarter past noon. "I really couldn't say, ma'am."

She took a sip. After a moment, she asked, "Are you planning on returning to school, once your mother gets better?"

"No, ma'am. I'll probably need to get a job."

"Doing what?" she asked.

"Laundry. Sewing. Maybe some farm work."

"Picking cotton?"

"Or tobacco," I told her. "Or both."

"My great-grandmother picked cotton," she said.

No shit, huh? This *was* the State of Georgia, wasn't it? This *was* the United States of America, right on? Was there a Negro within a thousand miles whose great-grandma hadn't picked cotton? I almost laughed out loud. But I caught myself, remembered why I was there, and let her go on.

"My great-grandfather was born on a plantation just about twenty miles from here," she said. "He was twenty years old when freedom came. My great-grandmother was fifteen. She was on a different plantation, out near Savannah. They didn't meet until after. My great-grandfather's name was Alfred, but people called him Buddy on account of him having so many good friends. My great-grandmother Sally Jean was like that, too. They were people you could be close to. People who'd let you get close. Some people who came out of slavery were the opposite. Scared to get too close because they knew how fast you could lose somebody. But my great-grandparents were brave that way. Brave in their hearts, you know?"

"Yes, ma'am."

"Buddy was a carpenter. That's what he did on the plantation, you know, built furniture and such. His master let him rent himself out on weekends, and he built up a clientele. When freedom came, a lot of the whites he'd worked for kept on giving him work, and he was able to make a good living. He was lucky. Most Negroes had to sharecrop, and that wasn't much better than slavery. Anyhow, he built himself a business. When he moved to Atlanta, he brought three of his friends with him, and some of their families, too. They all lived in the back of his store. He didn't have to do that, he could've left them behind. Kept more of the money for himself. But that was Buddy. Friends meant a lot to him, you know? And the business kept growing. The money started piling up. And somehow, with work and starting his own family, he still had time to play cards and shoot the shit. He loved a party.

"When he was old enough, my grandfather took over the business. He was just like his daddy. He loved a party, too. And just being with people, close, letting himself be known. He loved his friends as much as his family. Friendship made him happy. More than money. My grandparents and great-grandparents, they all knew what was important.

"My father had no interest in the furniture business. And his only interest in friends is in what they can do for him. But I've always known that Buddy and Granddaddy had it right. Money's great. But it doesn't beat good friends." She wasn't really talking to me. She hadn't been for a while. Her eyes were far away somewhere. Still, I'd hung on every word. Buddy reminded me of my own grandfather, except with money. Frederick Steele had so many friends, when he died they couldn't all fit in the church for his viewing and a fistfight broke out when somebody cut the line.

Mrs. Broussard was quiet now, staring off into the past. I didn't know if I should clear my throat or just wait in silence. I wished I'd said yes to that Coke. After while, she seemed to remember I was there again. "What was your favorite school subject, Doris?"

I was thrown by the switch in conversation. "My . . . uh . . . English, ma'am."

"So, Catie must've been your favorite teacher."

"Yes, ma'am."

"You *must* be her favorite student, for all the trouble she's going to for you." She sipped her drink. "You know Catie and I grew up together?"

"Yes, ma'am."

"We were the best of friends almost our whole lives. Until we weren't."

Something deep inside me—maybe Jesus, maybe my own intuition—told me not to ask any questions. For one thing, I wasn't raised to get up in grown folks' business. For another, I could tell Mrs. Broussard wasn't sober. If I started asking questions, I might get answers I didn't want. Then again? *I wanted them.* I couldn't help myself. "What happened?" I asked her.

"It's complicated."

The same thing Mrs. Lucas said.

"What so complicated 'bout it?"

Mrs. Broussard got up and walked over to the liquor cabinet. I watched as she poured herself another drink.

"I'm sure you know Catie used to have a husband," she said.

"Yes, ma'am. He passed away when I was still in school."

"Did you know him?" she asked.

I knew everybody in Millen. It wasn't big. But Robert Lucas had been a favorite son in our town. He'd gone to Morehouse, graduated at the top of his class, then come back to Millen to teach science and history at Burgess Landrum. When he became principal at thirty, he was the youngest one the school ever had. He coached football. He was kind, smart, and handsome—that rare one in twenty. "Everybody knew Mr. Lucas," I said. "He was a big man in Millen. And he was always nice."

"Robert *was* nice," she said. "And he loved Catie something fierce. She had a terrible time when he died. She couldn't get out of bed. She couldn't eat. She sure as hell couldn't make funeral arrangements. She asked me to come down to Millen to help. When I got there, she was sleeping, so I cleaned up the house and made some breakfast for her. When I heard her stirring, I went into her room. I asked if there was anything she needed. She kissed me and started taking off my clothes."

Hand to God, I considered getting up and walking out right then. But I couldn't move a muscle. I was gripped, as if by the hand of Lucifer himself.

"When Catie married Robert, she had to put away certain parts of herself," Mrs. Broussard said. She leaned forward and whispered, "The parts that liked to sleep with women."

"Sweet Jesus."

She laughed, throwing her head back. "Are you sure you want to hear this, Doris? Maybe I should stop right here. I take no pleasure in scandalizing nice church girls."

I knew that was a bald-faced lie but it didn't matter. I'd heard enough to know I had to hear more. I had to hear all of it. At the same time, I wanted to tell her to stop. She shouldn't be saying these things, even if they were true. But my first mind won out. "I can handle it," I told her.

"Well, what else is there to say?" she asked. "When Robert died, the parts Catie had put away came right back up to the surface. And, lucky me, there I was."

I tried to imagine Mrs. Lucas kissing this unpleasant, high-yellow woman on the mouth, but I couldn't. "So, you . . ."

"I gave her what she asked for. What she needed. And she took it. And took it. And took it again. I stayed a week in your little shit town, through the funeral. I was still there when her family and Julia and everybody else had come and gone. And in all that time, Catie never talked to me about Robert. Not once. Whenever I brought him up, she pulled me into her bedroom and shut me up by putting something in my mouth."

"What?"

She fell out laughing again. "Oh, *hun*. You *are* an innocent little thing, aren't you?" Then, pointing to my belly, "Well, not *so* innocent, I suppose."

My cheeks burned. But I couldn't dwell on it. I had to hear the rest.

"Anyhow. When she'd had enough, she sent me on home. When I called, she'd make excuses for why she couldn't talk. She returned none of my letters. We hadn't spoken ten words to each other since. Until she called to ask me if I knew anyone who would give you an abortion. She didn't even apologize when she called."

Her voice shook when she said that last part. My mouth went dry. I already knew they weren't on good terms when Mrs. Lucas called, because Mrs. Broussard had said so the night before, but hearing the whole story made it worse. I felt so many things: grateful to Mrs. Lucas for putting herself in such an awkward situation for me; ashamed to have asked so much of her; and shocked, hearing everything Mrs. Broussard was telling me—not just the juicy homosexual details, but the way Mrs. Lucas, who I knew to be a thoughtful person, had treated her friend in the years since.

"I don't understand why you helping me," I told Mrs. Broussard. "If you so mad at Mrs. Lucas."

"Catie's been my closest friend since I was five years old. Two years can't erase all that. If she needs something, and I can give it to her, I will. Besides, I missed her. I wanted to see her, any way I could. I hope that doesn't make you feel like a pawn, hun."

It did. But I was willing to be a pawn, so long as I didn't have to be pregnant anymore.

Looking satisfied with herself, she sat back down on the couch again. "Now you tell me something," she said. "Now that you know more about me than you ought to."

"Ma'am?"

"Who's the father? You got a horny little boyfriend back in Millen?"

"Naw."

"Did somebody force you? Is that why you want to get rid of it?"

"No, ma'am."

She frowned. "Well, it's got to be one or the other."

"It aint nobody, ma'am," I told her, in a tone I hoped would convey: *With all due respect, it's none of your damn business.*

Mrs. Broussard peered at me a moment, and I waited to see if she was going to push it. But right then Mrs. Lucas walked in. I tried to look normal, so she wouldn't suspect what we'd been talking about. I tried to smile, but I knew it looked like I needed to shit.

"Flowers are in the kitchen, Syl. Has the doctor called?"

Mrs. Broussard shook her head. "Not yet."

"How you holding up, Doris?"

"I'm alright." My voice sounded strange. And I was blinking too much, but I couldn't figure out how to blink less. *Get a grip, Doris!* I told myself. *This aint the first juicy business you ever heard!*

Mrs. Lucas didn't look the least bit worried that Mrs. Broussard might've told me something she shouldn't. And so I sat there, trying to keep my face from falling under the weight of these women's secrets passed on to me.

Pearl came in. "Sylvia? Carlton Locke is here," she said, just as a smiling man appeared. He was short and dark, with a full beard and the brightest white teeth I'd ever seen. He was wearing a three-piece suit. I found the loose thread on the sleeve of my blouse and tucked it under. *Another rich Negro,* I thought. I had no idea there was so many.

Mrs. Broussard got up and bounced over to him. "Well, isn't this a wonderful surprise!"

"What do you mean?" he asked. "I'm here for the party."

"Carlton, the party's not 'til eight."

"I know," he said. "I wanted to get here a little early, get a jump on the hors d'oeuvres."

"You're a mess!" she squealed, and they hugged one of those big hugs like men do, smacking each other on the backs. This man was three times Mrs. Broussard's girth, and for a second I worried he'd break her, but she came out the hug in one piece.

"Let me introduce you to my good friend Cate Lucas," she said. "And her niece, Doris. Y'all, this is Carlton Locke. Carlton's the president of the Licorice Theater Company."

The Licorice Theater Company traveled all over the South and the Northeast doing plays and musical shows for colored audiences. I'd read about them in *Ebony* and *Jet*.

"Pleasure to meet such lovely ladies as yourselves," Mr. Locke said. He had a feminine way about him, what I thought of then as sissified, a certain looseness in his hips and wrists, a flourish in his voice when he said *lovely*. I would've wondered about him on any old regular day, but after the conversation I'd just had with Mrs. Broussard, I didn't even wonder. There was just homosexuality in the air.

"You're just in time for lunch," Mrs. Broussard said.

"Lucky me! You know I love Pearl's cooking."

"Let's have a drink in the meantime."

Mr. Locke said he'd just got in from Charleston and wanted to freshen up from his travels first. Mrs. Broussard went to tell Pearl he was staying for lunch. When they were gone, Mrs. Lucas asked me about the conference. I'd forgot all about it. In fact, everything that happened earlier that day had faded from my memory—or run screaming from it—when Mrs. Broussard told me what she had. Now, I tried to remember the conference, what I'd felt being there. I told Mrs. Lucas about the workshop, how the students had been so focused. "I never seen nothing like it. They almost made me want to be a freedom fighter."

"What's stopping you?" she asked.

"You know it aint like this in Millen," I said. "It aint like here."

"Well, nowhere is like Atlanta," she said, sounding proud. "But Millen could use a freedom fighter."

"Sure, but not me."

"Why not you?"

"I don't know." I really didn't. I just knew, proud as I was of those kids, I didn't want to be one of them.

To get off the subject, I told Mrs. Lucas about the girls I'd met in the bathroom. "They was talking about men taking all the credit for the conference, leading all the workshops, even though women is doing most of the work."

"Sounds like a day that ends in 'y,'" Mrs. Lucas said.

"But it don't matter who get the credit," I said. "Good deeds ought to be done for they own sake."

"I agree," she said. "But if someone *is* going to get the credit, why should it always be men?"

"First Timothy say, 'I do not permit a woman to teach or to have authority over a man.'"

She gave me a funny look. "You don't believe that, do you?"

"Most teachers I know is women. So, that part don't make sense. But the other part, about women having authority over men. Most women don't, do they?"

"No," she said. "But does that mean we shouldn't?"

I didn't know any women who had authority over grown men. Not at school, or church, or anywhere else. I knew women who told their men what to do, as in *Nigger, get your socks up off the floor,* or *Stop drinking so much whiskey, it's Sunday for goodness' sake,* but those were wives and husbands, brothers and sisters. I didn't know women who told men what to do *outside* the house.

"If God wanted women to have authority over men," I said, "wouldn't he have given us some?"

Mrs. Lucas gave me a *real* funny look this time. "By that argument," she said, "God doesn't want colored people to have the same rights as white people. Just because something hasn't happened, doesn't mean it shouldn't. I think women are as smart and capable as men. So, why shouldn't we be out in front, leading the movement? I can't use a white restroom any more than a colored man can."

"Maybe," I replied. I still wasn't sure I liked the idea. It seemed unnatural. Ungodly. Uncouth, to boot. In fact, if it had been two days earlier, her argument would've sounded to my ears like some heathen talk. But compared to atheism and homosexuality? Women's rights didn't seem quite so outrageous. Besides, she had a point, I reckoned. Colored women worked hard. What exactly *was* wrong with us getting some of the shine, as long as the shine was being given out anyhow? I knew God wanted women to be modest in every way. The Bible made that plain. But, standing there now, with the space to ponder it good and hard and nobody telling me not to, I couldn't think of a reason why it ought to be that way. It suddenly seemed like a very strange thing for God to want.

Mr. Locke said he needed to make an important call, to check on ticket sale numbers for Licorice's upcoming show. Mrs. Broussard told him she was waiting for her own important call, but he could use the phone in the hall, which was a separate line. Five seconds after he left, I realized I couldn't be in a room with her and Mrs. Lucas without feeling like I might faint from the stress. So, I offered to help Pearl with lunch.

When I showed up in the kitchen, Pearl seemed bothered, like she didn't want my help.

"I got everything under control in here," she said. "Last thing I need is anybody in my way."

"Yes, ma'am," I said and turned to go. I reckoned I could hide out in the library for a while. But before I got out of the room, Pearl said, "Hold on a minute."

I turned back. She looked like she was thinking it over, considering things the nature of which I didn't have a clue. Finally, she sighed and said, "Well, alright. You can make the salad."

I made the salad, working in silence for a while. When I started slicing cucumbers, she said, "Cubes, child, not slices. Sylvia got something against sliced cucumbers." She said it like Mrs. Broussard and sliced cucumbers had been in a fistfight.

I did what she said and started cubing them. It took more effort this way, but that was good because it distracted my mind, kept me from looking up at the clock every twenty seconds, or thinking I heard the phone ring every other minute. After while, Pearl asked, "How old you, child?"

"Seventeen, ma'am."

"Same as my boy, Lil' Terrence," she said. "How much schooling you get before your ma got sick?"

"I finished tenth grade," I told her, wondering how she knew I'd left school. She must've been eavesdropping. Then I thought, maybe not eavesdropping so much as just listening. It would've been hard not to listen to the conversations happening around you all day long. That made me wonder what all Pearl knew. About Mrs. Broussard. About Mrs. Lucas. About me.

"Lil' Terrence been working since he was twelve," she continued. "Well, he *was* working. Until his last job got through. Now he say he want to be a musician. Play horns or piano in a jazz band."

"He any good?" I asked.

"Good as the next horn or piano player, I reckon. That enough?" She sucked her teeth, waved a hand to shoo the idea away. "I tell that hardheaded boy he need to get a job. Mr. Broussard say he can set him up with something at his construction company. Maybe even one of them highfalutin jobs, in the office. But Lil' Terrence talmbout, 'I don't read that well. I never move up in a place like that.' But I tell him, 'Through God all things possible.' "

If all things are possible through God, I thought, *why aint it possible for Lil' Terrence to play horns or piano in a jazz band?* I stopped cubing cucumbers and looked up at Pearl. I wanted to see if she'd heard herself, if the contradiction had landed on her at all. But she was shredding carrots like nothing.

Now, I'd been hearing "through God all things are possible" my whole life. Holy folks love to turn that phrase. But it struck me right then that I didn't know anybody who seemed to believe it. I didn't know anybody who didn't talk about life like it was small, its possibilities limited to whatever they, themselves, could imagine. Then *put on God.* And, I realized, I was no exception. The God I prayed to was offended when women didn't wear slips or told men what to do. He was so *unimagina-*

tive. Because *I* was so unimaginative. But here, in Atlanta, in Mrs. Broussard's house? That God seemed, not just petty, but suddenly very small. It stood out to me because the *only* thing that felt small here, besides me, was God.

The phone on the kitchen wall rang. My stomach jumped as Pearl went to answer it. "Broussard residence . . . Oh, hello, Julia."

I'd hoped it was the doctor, but my ears still perked up.

"Yes, she in," Pearl said. "I'll get her for you. One moment." She put down the phone and left the kitchen.

Soon, Mrs. Lucas came in. "You alright, Doris?" she asked when she saw me chopping.

"Yes, ma'am."

She smiled and picked up the phone. I pretended not to listen while hanging on every word.

"Afternoon, Julia," she said, easy, like she was greeting the mailman and not a woman who'd been on the cover of *Jet* magazine at least seven times. "Oh, we're about to have lunch." She didn't say anything for a while after that, and when I stole a glance at her she looked like she was thinking something over. "Yes," she said, "alright. I'll see you soon." And she hung up.

"Julia Avery coming for lunch?" I asked her.

She shook her head. "She just invited *us* to lunch," she said. "You and me. Would you like to go?"

Would I like to go? This *was* Julia Avery we were talking about. Who in their right mind wouldn't want to go to lunch with her? No offense to Mrs. Broussard, but it wasn't no toss-up. And, even though I was uneasy with the thought of what Miss Julia and her fingertip had been up to the night before, I wasn't any easier with what Mrs. Broussard had told me about her and Mrs. Lucas. I was surrounded by sinners, and it wasn't any getting around that, so I might as well try to enjoy myself.

"Alright," I told her. "Yes, ma'am, I'd like to go."

If Mrs. Broussard was the least bit offended when Mrs. Lucas asked if it was alright if we skipped lunch with her and Mr. Locke, she didn't show it. In fact, she offered us her Studebaker. "Carlton can take me anywhere I need to go before you get back."

Miss Julia's invitation was for two o'clock. "She stays up until three or four in the morning and sleeps until noon, so her meals are always late," Mrs. Lucas said. "At least, that's the way she used to be." I didn't mind because I still wasn't hungry. Mrs. Lucas suggested we go get our hair done in the meantime, that it'd be her treat, to keep my mind off the clock. "There's a salon in Sweet Auburn, close to where Julia's staying."

I'd read about Sweet Auburn in *Jet*. A long time ago, some wealthy man had called it "the richest Negro street in the world" and it stuck. There were lots of businesses there, all of them owned by colored people, and I was excited to see it. But I'd never been to a beauty parlor in my life. The colored women who did hair in Millen did it out of their homes, but I didn't go to them, either. It seemed a little silly to me, to pay somebody money to do your hair, when you could do it yourself, or have your ma do it. Besides, I couldn't afford it.

In Millen, Mrs. Lucas got her hair done at Mrs. Griffin's house, just like every other colored woman in our town who had money to spend on that kind of thing. Mrs. Griffin lived down the road from us, and I'd seen Mrs. Lucas going in there plenty of times with a scarf wrapped around her head, or coming out with a fresh press. Her favorite beauty shop in Atlanta, she said, was the Poro Beauty Parlor.

We parked on the street, near one end of Auburn, so we could walk most of the way up the avenue. We passed all kinds of shops—including a bakery with pies in the window, a bookstore with racks of magazines out front, and three different dressmakers—and Mrs. Lucas pointed out the office of the *Atlanta Daily World*. I must've known that a newspaper had to be printed *somewhere*, but I never thought about the where, or the how, or the by who.

"Who make the paper?" I asked Mrs. Lucas, looking up at the sturdy brick building.

"Well, a lot of people make it," she said. "Writers and editors and all that. I have a cousin who contributes articles about sports. But the paper's owned by a man named C. A. Scott."

"You know him?"

"Not really. I've met him once or twice."

I thought about this C. A. Scott person. I thought about Mr. Locke, too, and about Dexter's sister in Paris, and I wondered if God just made some Negroes luckier than others and, if he did, how he decided on who. Who to make smart or brave or full of a wanderlust strong enough to get them across an ocean. It didn't seem fair, somehow.

We walked farther up the avenue, passing shoeshine stands, a butcher, and even a little shop selling nothing but sweets. I had a few dollars, and I thought about going in to get treats for my brothers, but then I thought, considering the reason I was in Atlanta, maybe bringing home gifts was uncouth.

"This is the Royal Peacock Club," Mrs. Lucas said, as we passed a storefront with peacock feathers hanging in the windows, along with a poster advertising a performance by Aretha Franklin next month. "Robert and I used to come here for dinner and dancing whenever we came to Atlanta."

Julia Avery had said she'd been singing at the Royal Peacock when she collapsed. I wanted to go inside and see the stage where she'd sung, and where Aretha Franklin would sing next month, but the club wasn't open at that time of day.

We kept walking, past Big Bethel A.M.E., a church with a huge steeple that had a blue neon sign with the words *Jesus Saves* and a giant white cross on top of it.

"I grew up in this church," Mrs. Lucas told me. "Most of my family still goes here."

The Poro Beauty Parlor was on the same block as the church, in a six-story brick building with large, six-pane windows winking out at the street. Inside, the salon had a checkerboard floor pattern, soft pink chairs in the waiting room, framed posters of colored women with hot new hairdos, a row of dryers, and a pinkish glow to it all. A small woman with a big smile greeted us. "Cate Lucas! I thought that was you!" She was older than Mrs. Lucas, in her sixties, I reckoned, and her hair was pressed straighter than the righteous path to Jesus.

"Hey, Ella. How's business?"

"Booming," Miss Ella said. "Same as always. Beauty never goes out of fashion, does it?"

Mrs. Lucas introduced me as her niece, and Miss Ella

asked me what I wanted done today. I could see her eyeing my hair and I felt self-conscious. I didn't know what to ask for. I looked at Mrs. Lucas, and she must've seen the panic in my eyes, because she said, "What about a press and curl? Maybe sideswept in the front?" and made a wavy motion in front of my head with her hand.

Miss Ella nodded. "Mmm-hmm. That'd look just fine, wouldn't it?"

The first thing was a shampoo. I reclined with the back of my head over a sink while a skinny girl not much older than me drizzled shampoo in my hair and then massaged the foam through to my scalp and rinsed it out. Next, I was taken over to another chair and put under a dryer. After while, Mrs. Lucas was put under a dryer next to me. She smiled at me and patted my hand, then picked up a *Jet* and started flipping through it. I watched her profile for a moment, trying not to think about what Mrs. Broussard had told me. Of course, trying not to think about it only made me think about it more. So, I picked up an *Ebony* and started to read an article about Sammy Davis, Jr. But it was no use. I just couldn't concentrate.

When I was done under the dryer, a different woman led me over to a different chair. She pressed my hair, the hot comb sizzling as it did its work, then used a curling iron to bump the ends under. When she was finished, she spun the chair around so I could look in the mirror, and I stared at myself, in awe. I'd never looked so citified and sophisticated in my country-ass life.

When we left the beauty parlor, we headed down the street to Miss Julia's hotel. A woman walking by us smiled and said,

"Looking beautiful, ladies!" and I blushed, then felt silly. It wasn't like nobody had said anything nice to me before. I got my fair share of compliments in Millen. But this was Atlanta. To be called beautiful here felt different. It put a little pep in my step, right on.

Julia Avery had a two-room suite at the Royal Hotel. When she opened the door, and saw Mrs. Lucas standing there, her eyes sparkled the same way they had in Mrs. Broussard's dining room, and the name came out like a lyric again. "Caaate," she crooned, reaching for her hand, then stopped when she saw me standing there.

"Oh, I see you brought a friend along," Miss Julia said, her voice surprised and confused at the same time. That's when I knew she hadn't invited *us* to lunch.

"I hope it's alright," Mrs. Lucas said.

"Of course it's alright." But her eyes said something else. I reckoned I was intruding on something she'd meant to be private, that her fingertip had plans that didn't include me. But she was Southern, and if we know how to do anything, it's be hospitable, even while secretly wishing you'd turn around and take your ass on home. So, she took a step aside of the doorway and told us, "Y'all come on in," and damn if it aint sound sweet as pie.

The suite was something to behold. It was furnished with plush velvet sofas and chairs, in rich hues of emerald and ruby, arranged around a polished mahogany coffee table. The wallpaper had intricate gold peacock designs, and peacock feathers hung in frames on the walls. The chandelier caught the light coming in through the windows and threw it all around the room, casting a glow over everything, including a piano that stood in one corner. High ceilings and big windows made the place feel airy and spacious. "What a gorgeous room," Mrs. Lucas said, taking the words right out of my mouth.

"Is it?" Miss Julia asked.

"Don't you think so?"

She shrugged. "I suppose I'm sick of it, after being cooped up in here for two weeks."

"Well, why'd you leave Coretta's?" Mrs. Lucas asked.

"'Cause I was sick of being cooped up there, too," Miss Julia replied. "At least there're no screaming children here."

Mrs. Lucas walked over to the piano and ran her hand over the shiny wood.

"The piano's mine," Miss Julia said. "I had it brought in."

Mrs. Lucas picked up a sheet of paper off it. "You working on a new song?"

Miss Julia moved quick and took it from her. "Barely."

"Play it for us," Mrs. Lucas said, sounding excited.

But Miss Julia shook her head. "It's not ready for anybody to hear yet."

"Well, something else, then."

"Is this why you came?" Miss Julia asked, acting like she was offended. "To put me to work?"

"Of course not. I was just thinking how long it's been since I heard you play."

Miss Julia put the sheet music back on the piano. "Well, it'll be at least a little longer. Lunch'll be here soon. They're bringing it up from the restaurant downstairs."

"We could've gone down," Mrs. Lucas told her. "Especially if you're so tired of being cooped up in here."

"Oh, no," Miss Julia replied. "I was in there the other night with Coretta, and everybody and their mama wanted to say hello. I swear I didn't get more than three bites down in an hour and a half." She pursed her lips and shook her head at the thought. "Anyhow, it ought to be here any minute."

"Any minute's just what I need," Mrs. Lucas said. "Where's your restroom, Julia?"

"Just through the bedroom, on the left," Miss Julia told her, pointing that way.

When Mrs. Lucas had left the room, Miss Julia said, "Have a seat, darlin'," and I sat down on a green velvet couch. She picked up a pack of Benson & Hedges off the coffee table and lit a smoke. I watched her cheeks suck in as she pulled the fire from the lighter into the tip of the cigarette. I'd seen a cigarette being lit a thousand times, but somehow when Julia Avery did it, it was like nobody'd ever done it before. She was so cool. I wanted to ask her so many questions. About her singing and traveling and really anything about her life she was willing to tell me, even if I already knew about it from *Jet*. But I was too nervous to say a word. Every time I opened my mouth, nothing came out. Then I wondered what Lena would say if she knew I met *the* Julia Avery and didn't hardly say two words to her. She would've loved to have the chance I was having now.

"Miss Julia?"

She raised her eyebrows in my direction.

"Can I ask you a question?"

She nodded. "Go on."

"Well . . . I reckon you been everywhere," I said.

"I don't know about everywhere. But a lot of places, sure."

"What's your favorite place? Is it Paris?" I asked. "You been there?"

"Plenty," she said. "I sang at the Moulin Rouge just last winter."

I didn't know what the Moulin Rouge was, but it sure as shit sounded fancy. "Somebody told me it's a lot of colored folks there."

"A lot?" she asked, raising her eyebrows again, like it was news to her. "Well, if there are, I'm sure disappointed they didn't come to my show."

"What about James Baldwin and Josephine Baker?" I asked.

She thought about it. "Well, Jimmy's back in New York. But I get your meaning. Colored artists expatriating to France and all that?"

"Yes, ma'am. To get away from prejudice."

She bust out laughing. "*Get away from prejudice?* Darlin', prejudice is every damn where. Aint no getting away from it. They don't have segregation in the law, but they still find ways to keep us out when they want to. And even if they *do* want us around, it's not always for the right reasons."

And here I was thinking Paris was some kind of promised

land. Miss Julia must've seen the disappointment on my face. "I don't mean to rain on your parade," she said. "If I had to choose between the whites of France and the whites of the Jim Crow South, I'd choose Pierre and Jean-Claude over Bubba and Billy Bob any day. But France is like Sammy Davis, Jr.'s taste in women. Not near black enough. Paris *is* a damn good time, though, aint no doubt about that. And standing underneath the Arc de Triomphe, when it's all lit up, sure makes you feel like *somebody*." She smiled to herself. Then she reached over and grabbed a pen and a torn envelope from the coffee table and scrawled on it. Something about the way she did it reminded me of myself.

"What you writing, Miss Julia?" I asked her, hoping she wouldn't take it as nosy.

"What I was just saying, about the Arc de Triomphe," she told me, still writing. "I like the sound of it, and I don't want to forget it. I might put it in a song one day."

All these years, I've never really figured out how to describe my feelings when she said that. Much as I love to turn a phrase, some things live too deep in the soul for language to reach. Closest I can get is to say that, in that moment, I felt like I was the same as Julia Avery. Poor and ignorant and ordinary as I was.

"You alright, darlin'?" She was peering at me, worried. "You look like you're about to faint."

"No, ma'am," I told her. "I'm alright."

"Something else on your mind?" she asked.

There was so much on my mind, I didn't know where to begin.

"Well, come on," she said, replacing the cap on her pen. "You might never see me again. Now's your chance."

"How'd you know your life could be different?" I asked her. "I mean, when you was young, growing up in Alabama."

She took a drag off her cigarette and thought on it while she blew out the smoke. "My cousin Edythe got a scholarship to college when she was nineteen. When I saw her leave, when I saw her step up onto the train and wave goodbye to Heiberger, I knew leaving was possible. I never thought life in Alabama could be all there was. There was always a voice inside me, from the time I was a little girl, asking, 'What else?' When Edythe left, the voice got louder."

"A voice?" I asked.

"Mmm-hmm."

"What if there aint no voice?"

She looked at me a long moment, then said, "There's always a voice, darlin'. If you can't hear it, it's probably because there's too many other voices drowning it out." She took another pull off the cigarette and pointed at my hair. "Nice 'do, by the way."

Took me a second to catch up with the switch in conversation. "Oh, thank you, ma'am," I replied, touching it self-consciously. "Everybody sure do look sharp in Atlanta. I know I stick out like a pebble in a jewelry box here, even with this beauty parlor hairdo."

She laughed a little at that, and sort of looked me over again, like something about me was confusing to her. "Hold on a minute," she said. "You're not from Atlanta?"

"No, ma'am," I told her. "I'm from Millen."

She nodded her head. "I see."

"We aint got nowhere near as many fancy Negroes in colorful clothes as they got here," I said. "Everywhere I turn, look like a garden blooming."

She peered at me, her face a mix of interest and amusement. "You *sure* got a knack for describing things, girl."

"Thank you, Miss Julia." I hadn't been trying to impress her—I was so starstruck, I hadn't even thought to—but I felt proud that I had. I sat there, grinning.

"But it's funny," she said. "I could've sworn all Cate's kin was from Atlanta."

If a grin was a potato, it would've hit the floor with a thud when it dropped off my face. I opened my mouth to say something, but nary a damn word came out.

Mrs. Lucas walked back in the room. When she saw Miss Julia peering at me, and me sitting there in dumb silence, she looked worried. "What are y'all talking about?"

I decided that if Miss Julia was on to us, she was going to have to say so herself. I waited. But she just smiled and said, "I was noticing Doris's way with words."

Mrs. Lucas beamed. "She sure can turn a phrase, can't she?"

There was a knock on the door. "That'll be lunch," Miss Julia said, and went to answer it, opening it wide for a waiter in a crisp white uniform, who rolled a cart in. The cart held trays covered with silver domes, pitchers of water and lemonade, shiny silverware, and white napkins folded to look like little pyramids. The waiter rolled it all to the center of the room and grinned. "Here you go, Miss Avery. Anything else I can get for you?"

"This'll do me just fine," she told him, slipping money into his hand.

He took it and thanked her, but he didn't leave. He kept standing there, grinning at her.

"You need something, hun?" she asked. "An autograph?"

"We aint supposed to ask," he said, taking a pen and a pad of paper out of his back pocket faster than a cowboy unslinging his gun in a Western, "but . . . if it aint too much trouble . . ."

She took the pen and paper and signed her name. She handed it back to him, then put a hand on his arm and walked him over to the door. When she closed it, he was still standing there, grinning. The boy had teeth for miles.

Under the shiny domes were trays of fried chicken, candied yams, greens, and warm bread. To my surprise, the appetite I couldn't find at Mrs. Broussard's poked its head out and started buttering a roll.

While we ate, the old friends talked. Mrs. Lucas talked about teaching. Miss Julia talked about being on tour. I kept waiting for them to talk about old times, the way they had at Mrs. Broussard's the night before, but they never did. And I kept looking for something—a glance, a touch, a word—between them that would prove what I thought I saw last night, but that never happened, either. Still, I reckoned just because they weren't letting me see it, didn't mean it wasn't there.

"I love being on tour," Miss Julia told us. "I always do. But I was hoping to have this song finished first. I can't ever write anything on the road."

Mrs. Lucas nodded. "I know."

"It's nearly done, but there's a few things just not coming together—" She suddenly stopped and looked at me. "Come to think of it, I could use somebody good with words. I'd ask you, Cate, but you might be suspicious of the subject matter."

"Meaning what?" Mrs. Lucas asked.

But Miss Julia was already getting up and crossing the room to the piano.

If I'd understood what was happening, I would've panicked at the thought that Julia Avery believed I could help her with a song. But my mind was a beat behind as she grabbed the sheet of paper from the piano then came and sat down again.

"It's a song about a brokenhearted woman," she said. "I want to say her lover has left her, moved on, you know? The way I wrote it, it goes: 'You set me aside like an unfinished book.'" She shook her head. "But it don't work. It's too cumbersome or . . . *something*," she said, looking in my direction.

That's when I realized she was asking me. *She was asking me.* For a moment, I went blank. And then, like a firebolt from the heavens, struck by Jesus himself, it hit me. "You forgot me like a song from last summer."

Miss Julia's eyes got wide. "'You forgot me like a song from last summer,'" she repeated, almost a whisper. "Shit, girl. That's *good*."

She looked at Mrs. Lucas, who looked like she might fall out of her chair, then back at me. "Maybe I'll use that," she said. "Would you mind?"

"No, ma'am. I don't mind," I told her.

The rest of lunch was a blur. Miss Julia and Mrs. Lucas

talked and ate, and I must've talked and ate with them. I must've been excited that the famous Julia Avery might use my words in a song, even if it was just a maybe. I must've kept looking for a certain kind of glance or touch between them, and if I saw one, I must've prayed to Jesus for their souls. But I can't say any of that for sure, because all I remember is sitting there thinking about the voice in my head that I couldn't hear.

"You alright, Doris?" Mrs. Lucas glanced over at me in the passenger seat of Mrs. Broussard's Studebaker, as we drove back to Collier Heights. "You're mighty quiet, sugar."

I told her what Miss Julia had told me, about the voice, and other voices drowning it out.

"What do you hear when it's all quiet?" Mrs. Lucas asked me.

"It aint never all quiet. Unless I'm in the outhouse, and sometime not even then, if Bud follow me in there." The rare times it *was* all quiet, or when I could at least block out the noise, I mostly just turned phrases in my head, thought up interesting or funny ways to put things, and wrote them down. But I didn't reckon that was about to get me anywhere, so I kept it to myself. "Miss Julia's voice made her think there was something else for her, outside Alabama," I said. "Made her want to go find that something else."

"Is there somewhere you want to go?"

"I aint sure. It aint so much the going as the choosing to go,

I reckon. It's strange, but all of a sudden I feel like I'm gon' bust if I can't choose *something* for myself."

"Aren't you doing that already?" she asked. "Isn't that why we came to Atlanta? Having an abortion is your choice."

"Yes, ma'am. But what choices do I get after? When I go back home, I won't be pregnant no more, God willing, but everything else gon' be the same."

"And you don't want everything to be the same?"

I thought again about Pearl, and all those other church folks who talked about what was possible through God, but dreamed nothing more than what could fit through the eye of a needle and still have room for a *hallelujah*. And I realized I didn't want to be like them anymore. "No, ma'am."

"How do you want things to be different?"

"I don't rightly know. Out the blue, I got this yearning inside me for something else. But it's hard to know what it could be, and it's harder to think how I'd ever get to it, even if I knew what it was. 'Don't waste time daydreaming, Doris. It's washing to get done.' That's what Ma always say."

"Maybe the voice in your head, the one that's drowning out your own voice, is hers."

"Ma aint to blame," I said, feeling protective.

"I don't mean any offense to your mother," Mrs. Lucas said. "Everybody loves Babe, and I'm no exception. And I don't mean to single her out, either. Most colored girls have more voices telling them what they can't do than what they can. A lot of those voices speak in the name of love, or what they believe is love. And maybe it is love. But there's a whole heap of fear piled up on top of it, too." She sighed. "I've been a teacher for ten years and one thing I know is that a pupil never gets anything they don't believe they *can* get. Most teachers will tell you that their favorite thing is when a pupil who's been struggling with an idea suddenly *gets it.* The look on a child's face when it all comes together is a big part of why I became a teacher, too. But there's another look that comes before that one, when a pupil who thinks they *can't* get it—that they're not smart or hardworking enough—finally *believes* that they can."

"How?" I asked her. "What make them believe that?"

"I do," she told me, and smiled. "A good teacher does. The great news for you, Doris, is that you already believe."

"Ma'am?"

She nodded. "I could see it in your face just now when you told me what you asked Julia and what she answered. Despite all the voices telling you that you shouldn't, here you are asking questions, here you are trying to dream up something for yourself. You may not know the what or the how, but the believing is all over you, sugar."

I shook my head. But even as I did, I realized she was right. The moment I'd seen Miss Julia scrawling on that envelope; the moment I'd felt her and me were the same, little sense as it made; the moment I'd seen some tiny part of myself in the enormity of her; I'd started to believe, for the first time, that my life *could be different,* somehow. And, once I believed, without even planning on it, I started to look for the what and the how, sho'nuff.

"Do you think Mr. Locke would give me a job?" I asked Mrs. Lucas. "Traveling with his theater company?"

"Is that what you want? To travel?"

"Maybe." The truth was, I'd never thought about leaving Millen, and even now that I was thinking about it, I didn't completely love the idea. But it *was* something different. And that felt like a start.

11

hen we got back to Mrs. Broussard's, she was waiting for us in the front hallway with a worried look on her face. "Syl? What's wrong?" Mrs. Lucas asked, before we'd even made it all the way inside.

Mrs. Broussard pulled us into the dining room, and we huddled around her. "The doctor called," she said, her voice barely more than a whisper. "I'm afraid he won't be able to do it."

My stomach churned. "He won't? Why . . . why not?"

"I'm not exactly sure, hun," she replied. "These arrangements can be quite . . . precarious."

I knew it was rude, but all I could do was stare at her, stunned.

Mrs. Lucas checked her watch. "Well, we should head home before it gets too late."

Home, I thought. *And still pregnant. Right back where I started.*

"Home? Don't be ridiculous, Catie. I'm sure I'll be able to find someone else by tomorrow."

"And what if you can't find someone, Sylvia?" Mrs. Lucas

asked. "No. I think we should go back to Millen and find a granny midwife."

"Don't be ridiculous," Mrs. Broussard said again, even though there was nothing ridiculous about it. She started getting all fidgety, wringing her hands. It suddenly dawned on me then that she'd been lying all this time. That the doctor had canceled long ago, maybe yesterday, but she hadn't wanted Mrs. Lucas to leave. Or maybe . . .

"Was it ever a doctor at all?"

She looked at me, blinked. "Of course there was a doctor. There *is* a doctor. What are you even thinking, child?"

"You made it all up."

Her high-yellow face turned red as the devil. "That's a *lie,*" she said, her voice low and serious. "I would never do something so dishonest. Why would I?"

To get Mrs. Lucas here, I wanted to say, but I couldn't get up the nerve.

"There *was* an appointment. But Herman called this morning and said he couldn't do it."

I could feel Mrs. Lucas bristle beside me. "*This morning?*"

"I didn't tell you because I didn't want Doris to worry," Mrs. Broussard said, still wringing her hands. "And, besides, I'm confident I can find someone else."

I didn't know what to believe. Part of me wanted to smack her. Another part of me wanted to beg her to fix it.

Mrs. Lucas put her hand on my arm. "Doris, let me have a moment in private with Mrs. Broussard."

I left, but only into the hallway, where I could still hear everything.

"Is she right?" Mrs. Lucas asked. "Did you lie? Was it to get me here?"

I was surprised that Mrs. Lucas had been thinking the same thing as me.

"No." Just like that. Without a moment's hesitation. "What have I ever done to make you think so poorly of me, Catie? Have I ever been anything but a loyal friend to you?"

"I told Doris you would help her, Sylvia. I promised her it would all be alright."

"And it will be. I already called another doctor I know. I'm sure I'll hear from him soon."

"And if not?"

"Then I'll talk to my father. He knows every colored doctor in Georgia."

"Your father would never approve of what we're doing. He thinks raising children is all women are good for."

"He's mellowed quite a bit in his old age. You haven't been around to see it. If I ask him, if I sit him down and tell him it's important to me, I think he'll help. He's back from Nashville next week."

"Next week?"

My stomach churned again. I felt like I might lose the fancy hotel lunch after all.

"We should've just stayed in Millen," Mrs. Lucas said, sounding defeated, "gone to a granny midwife there."

"You told me Doris didn't want to do that."

"I should've insisted."

"But you didn't, did you?"

There was a pause. Then Mrs. Lucas asked, "Meaning what, Sylvia?"

"Meaning you wanted to come, and helping this girl was the excuse you needed. Maybe you miss Atlanta more than you let on."

Another pause. I wished I could see Mrs. Lucas's face. "If that's true," she said, "it only makes me *more* responsible for bringing Doris all the way here and getting her hopes up for nothing."

"It's *not* for nothing. I *will* help her. I promised you I would. When have I ever broken a promise to you?"

I didn't hear the answer, because I had to run to the bathroom and throw up. Knelt in front of the toilet, I thought about how I'd only just let myself believe there might be something else for my life. And now I might not be able to do much of anything but be somebody's mama after all.

When I got through throwing my guts up, I went out on the front porch for some air. The afternoon was warm, the sun spectacular in the blue sky, a perfect Georgia day. It made me wonder if God was messing with me. Mrs. Lucas came out.

"Doris, I want to apologize again for all of this confusion with Sylvia," she said. "I know she can come off brash, but that's mostly because she didn't get enough attention as a child. And she's lonely out here in Collier Heights, even if you'd never suspect it. I know her, so I can see it. She's been a loyal friend to me most of my life. She's not dishonest, I promise you; she just has a hard time accepting that you can't always fix everything with money and status. I really don't think she'd lie just to keep us here. I believe she's trying to help. I do trust her."

"You shouldn't trust her," I said, then right away wished I hadn't. The last thing this whole mess needed, the last thing *I* needed, was to open a homosexual can of worms.

"Why do you say that?" she asked me.

I didn't answer. I couldn't think of a damn thing to say.

Mrs. Lucas peered at me. Her whole body was tense. "Doris," she began, then stopped. She swallowed. "Did Sylvia say something to you?"

I shook my head. "No, ma'am."

"Are you sure? Because she's been drinking all day and . . . maybe you misunderstood something she said—"

"Yes, ma'am, I must've misunderstood!"

Her jaw tightened. "What did Sylvia say?"

Lord Jesus, please open up a hole in the ground and let me fall into it. Amen.

"*Tell me,*" Mrs. Lucas demanded.

I felt sick to my stomach again. I knew I had to tell her. I knew I couldn't just keep standing there silent, staring at her like a dumbass.

"She said before you married Mr. Lucas, you used to be . . . *that way,*" I said, keeping my voice low even though there was no one near enough to hear us. "She said when Mr. Lucas died, she came to visit and you . . . I don't know. I must've misunderstood, like you said."

But I knew I hadn't misunderstood, and she knew I knew it. She looked scared. I felt awful for not keeping my fool mouth shut.

"I aint believe her," I said, desperate to give her a way out. "She was drinking, right on. Pastor Mills say liquor is the devil's refreshment. I aint fool enough to believe nothing she said after that much rum." I tried to laugh but it came out more like a cough. I could tell she wasn't buying a word of it. She swallowed again and that's when I realized she was trying not to cry. I couldn't bear it. I was out of lies, so I gave up and told the truth. "You aint got to worry. I won't never tell nobody."

Her bottom lip trembled. She didn't say anything, just stared past me out at the road.

I didn't say anything, either, at first. I reckoned I'd said enough. But, after while, I just couldn't take it anymore.

"I won't tell nobody," I said again. "Don't you believe me? I swear to God, Mrs. Lucas. To Jesus. On my ma's life. If I'm lying, may the Good Lord strike me down. May I burn in hellfire for all eternity. May the devil himself—"

"It's alright, Doris," she said, finally. "I believe you."

I was sure relieved. But she didn't look any less worried. She sat on the porch swing and patted the seat beside her. I sat down.

"Doris, do you know what would happen if people found out about . . . what Sylvia told you? People back home?"

"I reckon there'd be talk."

"*Talk* would be the least of it," she said. "I would lose my job, Doris. I would lose friends, family. I've seen all those things happen to people, and worse. It's hard to trust anyone with that kind of a secret."

"Yes, ma'am."

"Still . . ."

Still?

"There is some relief in having you know. Well, maybe not relief, exactly. But it makes things easier."

I wasn't sure what she meant. And, besides, up until that moment, I was ready to drop the subject. I was ready to drop it and leave it and never mention it again, out of respect. But soon as I heard the word *relief,* I decided it was worth trying to get some juicy details.

"When you were younger, did you and Mrs. Broussard used to be . . ." I hesitated, realizing I didn't know the right words to talk about women that way. The words I would've used for a relationship between a man and a woman—*sweethearts, steadies*—didn't seem to fit. *Lovers* had always sounded salacious to me, like something Jesus would disapprove of, no matter who was involved. Luckily, Mrs. Lucas didn't need me to finish the sentence to know what I was getting at. She looked in my eyes, and I could tell she was deciding whether to lean into the relief, or step back into the secret. It was a long moment and I worried she'd choose the secret. *Jesus, my Savior, King of Kings, Lord of Lords, please keep her talking long enough for me to hear about some of the wicked things women do in bed together. Amen.*

"We were close," she said. "When we were teenagers."

"How close?" I knew I was pushing it but, hand to God, I couldn't stop myself! "Kissing-on-the-mouth close?"

She didn't say yes. But the fact that she didn't say no emboldened me.

"Getting-naked-and-kissing-on-the-mouth close?"

"Doris!" she said, looking shocked, embarrassed, and taken aback to boot.

I'd gone too far. Like Lot's wife turning back to look at the fires of Sodom and Gomorrah, I'd gone too damn far. "I'm sorry!" I said. "It's just that ever since I saw you with Julia Avery last night, I can't stop thinking about what women do together."

She peered at me. "What do you mean?"

"Well, Lena said one woman acts like the man, but with fingers instead of a—"

"Doris!" She was plumb mortified now. "I am your *teacher*."

"Not no more," I reminded her.

"Still. It wouldn't be appropriate for me to talk to you about things like that."

"Who gon' know?"

"I'll know."

"Well, sho," I said, "but who else?"

"*Doris*. Please don't ask me those kinds of questions."

"Yes, ma'am. Alright." *Damn it,* I thought. *I was so close.*

"I was asking what you meant about Julia," she said.

"Oh. Well, I thought I saw something the night she come by here with Mrs. King."

"Something like what?"

"I don't know, exactly. Just how you looked at each other." I was embarrassed to say the other part, about how Miss Julia had touched her. Even though it happened right in front of me, it seemed so private, like something I shouldn't have seen.

Mrs. Lucas sort of laughed and shook her head. "And here I was thinking I was acting restrained."

"I'm sorry, ma'am. I don't mean to embarrass you."

"I'm not embarrassed," she said. That vexed me because it was one of the few times I could remember when a woman's desire didn't feel wrapped up in shame, either her own shame or somebody else's on her behalf.

"Julia does bring something out in me," she added.

"Are you in love with her?" I asked, and then found myself surprised by the question. I never imagined that kind of love between women. What little I'd heard about women, or men, who were "that way," was always all about sex. Pastor Mills preached against sodomy, not love. And since I'd seen Mrs. Lucas with Julia Avery, all I'd been able to think about was what they did in bed. But Mrs. Lucas was a woman who teared up reading poetry out loud. To imagine her in love with anyone should've been easy. Besides, if through God all things were possible, why not that kind of love between women?

Mrs. Lucas seemed surprised by my love question, too, and I thought she wasn't going to answer, that she'd say it was inappropriate and that'd be that. You could've buttered my ass and called me toast when she nodded and said, "I was in love with her at Spelman. She said she was in love with me. But Julia's always had plenty of women and I never really felt sure where I stood with her."

I sat unmoving, dead silent, not wanting to do anything that would stop her from telling it.

"One of the reasons I married my husband was that I knew he was devoted to me. He was like Julia in a lot of ways. He was charming. Popular. But when we met, it was as if no other woman existed for him. I liked that. I thought I needed it. So, I married him and I left Atlanta. And Julia. And the uncertainty."

"Was her heart broke?" I asked, barely a whisper because I didn't want to snap her out of whatever state of mind she was in that was making her tell me all this. I found it thrilling, the idea that my English teacher could have broken the heart of the famous Julia Avery.

But Mrs. Lucas laughed. "Julia? Heartbroken?"

"Was last night the first time you seen her since you left?"

"No. The first time I saw her again was when Robert and I went to one of her shows. We'd been married ten years by then. I found out she was performing in Atlanta, and I had this overwhelming need to see her. Just to see her, nothing else. But Robert insisted on letting her know we were there. She asked us backstage to say hello before the show started. When she found out we were all the way back in the ninth row, she gave us new seats, second row center. I remember wanting her to look at me from the stage, to look out and see me, if only for a moment, but she was in full performance mode, making eyes at everyone. Then near the end of the show, she said she was going to sing a song for someone she'd loved, a kind of a fantasy song because it hadn't worked out in real life. And then she started singing 'Come Rain or Come Shine,' from *St. Louis Woman,* and she looked at me, right into my eyes. 'I'm gonna love you, like nobody's loved you . . . ' "

I remembered Dexter playing the Ray Charles version of that same song last night.

"I told myself that if she asked me," Mrs. Lucas went on, "I would leave my husband right then and there and follow her wherever she wanted me to go. And then the show ended, and we went on home.

"After that, I saw her sometimes, if she happened to be in town when I came to Atlanta to visit my folks or Sylvia or other friends. But only in passing while Robert was alive. About a year after he died, I was visiting a friend in Memphis and I saw Julia at a party, and we talked for hours. It shocked me how fast all the feelings came rushing right back. The excitement, the comfort of being so close to someone who knows you so deeply. And then that same uncertainty. Wondering if it all meant more to me than it did to her, because maybe she had another woman waiting for her at home. Or several. I hated that feeling almost as much as I did when I was twenty, so I made up some excuse and I left. Last night was the first time I've seen her since then."

I'd been holding my breath the whole time, through the whole story, but I had to let it out to say, "You seemed happy to see her."

"I'm always happy to see her," Mrs. Lucas replied. "It's always good, always easy, as long as I don't let myself get too caught up."

I wanted to ask what exactly "caught up" meant but I suspected it had something to do with sex and was off-limits.

"I don't know what's gotten into me," she said. "I never told anyone about that show, about that song, besides Sylvia. I don't know why I'm telling you all this."

"I can keep a secret," I told her.

She looked at me, in my eyes. "Doris," she said, "if I'd had any idea Sylvia would be so indiscreet, I never would have brought you here. I never wanted you to have to keep secrets for me."

"But I *want* to."

"Why?" she asked.

"To protect you."

"It isn't your job to protect me."

"Sure it is. Aint we supposed to protect the people we love if we can?"

She hugged me. I wrapped my arms around her waist and held on. I wished she was my ma. Shamed as I am to admit it, because it's disrespectful to my real ma. But Mrs. Lucas seemed to know, better than anyone I'd ever met, how to love people. How to see them exactly as they were and love them that way. I wanted to love her back the same.

When we let go, I asked, "What now?" The thought of going home, still pregnant, was agonizing.

"I don't believe Sylvia would lie just to keep us here," Mrs. Lucas said, "if she didn't really think she could find another doctor by tomorrow. Maybe it's foolish of me, but I do believe she's trying to help, as much as it baffles me that she would tell you about us, drunk or not."

"I don't think it was just the liquor," I told her. "She real sad."

Now Mrs. Lucas did look embarrassed. I thought about dropping it, letting her off the hook. I was mad at Mrs. Broussard, anyhow, so why should I care? But it seemed out of character for Mrs. Lucas to behave so coldheartedly. I wanted to know why.

"How come you aint talk to her for so long?" I asked.

Mrs. Lucas closed her eyes and let out a long breath. Then she opened her eyes and just sort of stared off into nothing for a few moments. Finally, she said, "When Robert died, the very first thing I felt was shock. But the thing after that? Was relief."

"Relief?" I asked, surprised.

"I thought about Atlanta, and everything and everyone I'd left behind here when I married Robert. And I felt relieved that now I could get it all back. When I called Sylvia, I wanted her help making arrangements for the funeral. But what I didn't tell her was that I wanted her to come and take me home. What happened between us over those days happened because I was trying to be another version of myself, the Cate I was before Robert, the Cate I'd left here in Atlanta. But everything changed when Robert went into the ground. Turned out, what I thought was relief was really only grief in disguise. Grief is like that. It fools you, in all kinds of ways. Once Robert was buried, it hit me like a truck. Those first couple of days after the funeral, I kept thinking I was going to wake up from a nightmare, and turn over, and he'd be right there, reaching out for me. I wanted him back. I cried out to a God I didn't even believe in, to let me have him back. I pushed away any thought of Atlanta, any thought of leaving Millen. I sent Sylvia home. I never *decided* not to talk to her. When she called, I just felt so much guilt for having wanted to be that other Cate again. For having betrayed Robert by wanting to leave. It took a long time to forgive myself for that. And even longer to realize I had nothing to forgive. Robert was dead. I loved him but he was dead. And I was alive. But by then, it had been a year and a half since I'd spoken to Sylvia. She'd stopped calling me. And I felt too ashamed of myself to call her after all that time. Then when you asked for my help . . . Well, Sylvia thinks you were the excuse I needed to get back here, and I guess she's right."

She sighed. "I owe her an apology. But I don't even know where to start."

We sat there swinging gently for a few moments. Then Mrs. Lucas said, "None of this is your problem, is it? If you want to go home, I'll take you. It's too late to travel safely now but I can take you first thing in the morning."

"I aint sure what to do," I told her.

"I'll let you think about it," she said, and went on back in the house.

I got up and started pacing. I wanted to scream. And cry. Pacing made feel like a caged-up animal, so I decided to walk.

Shade trees lined Mrs. Broussard's street—oaks and maples with some elms and sycamores—their leaves turning golden and crimson in the autumn sun. A lot of the houses were set back from the street by spacious, manicured lawns dotted with dogwoods and magnolias. The lawns were bordered by low hedges, azalea and camellia bushes, or fences that let in glimpses of the flower gardens, fountains, and even statues that decorated the front yards. It was all so pretty, and it was hard to stay mad, looking around and knowing colored folks owned everything out there. Most of the homes had wide porches but near all of them were empty. Maybe rich Negroes preferred to be inside with all their belongings. Thinking about rich Negroes reminded me again of Mrs. Broussard and then it *wasn't* hard to stay mad.

I heard a horn honk, and when I turned and looked, I saw a car pulling up alongside me. It wasn't Mrs. Broussard's car, and I didn't know anybody else in Atlanta, so I got suspicious right off. I kept walking, and the car kept driving slow beside me, and honked again. Finally, I stopped and peered in the window; I saw a man looking out at me, smiling with a gap between his front teeth, the hairs on his chest peeking out of his unbuttoned gaucho shirt.

"Hey there, Miss Doris," he said. "You 'member me?"

It was a dumb question. Of course I remembered him. It hadn't been but a few hours since we met and I wasn't senile, for pity's sake. Besides, he was too fine to forget.

"Sure," I said. "Elgin, aint it?" I knew it was Erik, but I didn't want him to think he'd made that much of an impression on me.

He smiled wider and said, "Close enough," and I told myself that if I ever did get married, it ought to be to the kind of man who didn't expect me to remember his name. The kind of man who knew I had more important things to think about than him.

"What you doing walking around out here by yourself?" he asked me. "You lost? Can I help you find your way?"

"I aint lost," I said. "I just aint sure what to do with myself." Truth was, the moment I saw him, I thought of some things I'd like to do. "What you fixing to get up to?" I asked him, casual as could be.

"My aunt live over yonder," he said, gesturing with a nod in the direction he'd come from. "I just got through helping her out with some things. Now I'm gon' head over to the Greenes' for a spell."

He said, "the Greenes'" like I had any way of knowing

what or who the Greenes were. When I stared at him, blank, he said, "They a family outside town we been looking out for."

"Guard duty?" I asked.

He nodded. "They got on the wrong side of the Klan."

"Aint no side of the Klan a Negro can get on *but* the wrong side," I reminded him.

He laughed. Then he said, "Aint never no trouble this time of day but I goes anyway, just in case. You can come on with me if you want. Long as you don't mind guns."

12

We drove for half an hour, through town and out to where the homes were more spread out, and arrived at a small house surrounded by an acre or so of land that was planted with vegetables and peanuts. A man was standing on the front porch, leaning against the railing, with a shotgun hanging from a strap over his shoulder.

I *didn't* mind guns. In fact, after sitting in Nonviolence Workshop 6, and watching those kids getting cigarette smoke blown in their faces, I'd wondered if the other side of the movement—the side that had the guns—might be a better match for me. I know it sounds crazy, churchgoing and God-fearing as I was, but the idea of turning the other cheek aint do nothing for me. I just couldn't cotton to it. So when Erik opened his trunk and took out his shotgun and said, "You want this or the pistol?" I took the shotgun before he finished the question. I'd never fired a pistol, hadn't ever had a reason to, but last fall I'd dropped the biggest buck you ever saw with Daddy's shotgun.

9

We drove to a neighborhood that looked nothing like Mrs. Broussard's, full of modest houses and apartment buildings, some of them run-down. Dexter pulled into a small parking lot in front of a small apartment complex and turned off the car. He leaned over and opened the glove box, his hand brushing my knees, and took out a pistol.

"What that for?" I asked, startled.

"I'm robbing somebody," he said. Then, seeing my expression, he laughed. "You should see your face right now. I'm only jiving. I'm returning this."

We got out the car, and he tucked the pistol in his waistband. I followed him up a few concrete steps and down a walkway to a door marked *27.* I could hear a harmonica playing from somewhere close by, and a man singing in between the mouth harp's notes, an old blues tune: "Boogie Chillen." Dexter knocked on the door and, after while, a lock clicked and the door opened. A suspicious face poked out. Then, seeing us, the face relaxed and opened the door all the way.

"Dex," said the man, extending his hand. "How you been, brother?"

Dexter slapped him five. "Hey, Brother Maurice. I been alright. How about you?"

"Shit. You know."

Dexter nodded. "Charlie here? I brought back his pistol."

"He out back. Come on through." The man stepped aside. His eyes were on me as I followed Dexter through the door.

Inside, the apartment was small but neat. We passed through a living room and then a kitchen, then out through the back door, all the time moving toward the sound of the harmonica. Finally, we stepped out onto a porch, where a man who looked to be in his late twenties or early thirties sat smoking a cigarette and cleaning a shotgun. A younger man, in his early twenties, was leaning against the porch railing, playing the harmonica. He was tall and lean, with pecan-colored skin. He was wearing a gaucho shirt with the buttons undone, so I could see the curly hairs on his chest. He looked at me over top of the instrument as he played, and his eyes were bright.

When the older man saw us, he set down the rag he was using to wipe down the gun. "What happened to you?" he asked Dexter, nodding toward the blood on his shirt. The younger man stopped playing and put the instrument into his shirt pocket.

"Nothing," Dexter replied. "Just a nosebleed." He reached into his waistband and pulled out the pistol. Holding it by the barrel end, he handed it over.

"I reckon you aint need to use it?" the man, who I figured was Charlie, asked.

The man on the porch waved to us as we walked up to the house.

"Howdy, Benny," Erik said. "Everything quiet around here?"

Benny nodded. "No trouble a'tall." He looked at me, then back at Erik. "If I'da known you was bringing a date, I'da picked you some flowers. Laid out a picnic blanket."

"This my friend Doris. She here to help."

Benny eyed me up again, longer this time. "She don't look like she got it in her to put a bullet in a Klansman ass."

Erik sucked his teeth. "Nigger, please. How many Klan you ever shot?"

"You don't know what I done, Erik."

"I know what you *aint* done."

They stared at each other, both looking ready to fight. Then they fell out laughing. It was a familiar routine, and I wondered why men always did it. Seemed like it woulda got tiring after while.

Benny put his arm around Erik's shoulders. "Missed you, boy. How you been?"

"Not too bad, Benny. You know how it is, man."

"I surely do."

The screen door opened, and a woman poked her head out. "I thought I heard you out here, Erik."

He tipped his hat to her. "Howdy, Miss Elaine. I brung a friend along. I hope it's alright. I reckoned you wouldn't mind the extra eyes."

She looked at me. "I don't mind the extra gun, neither. What's your name, hun?"

"Doris, ma'am."

"Pleased to meet you, Doris. I'm Mrs. Ralph Greene. You can call me Miss Elaine."

"Yes, ma'am."

"You know how to shoot that gun?"

"Yes, ma'am."

"Who taught you?"

"My daddy."

"That's good," she said. "More girls ought to know how to shoot. Aint *nobody* less safe in this world than a colored girl. You hear me?"

I nodded.

"Well, thank you for coming."

"Yes, ma'am. I'm glad to help."

She turned back to Erik. "I been nervous all morning. All this Klan nonsense. It takes a toll, you know?"

Erik nodded. "Yes, ma'am."

"It's almost five-thirty," Benny said, checking his watch. "Ralph get off at seven, so he ought to be home in 'bout a hour and a half."

When Benny was gone, Erik took his place standing at the railing, and I sat in a rocking chair nearby, the shotgun laid across my lap. Looking back at it, I should've been scared, out in who-knows-where, betting the Klan wouldn't show up in daylight. But I wasn't scared. Not too much, anyhow. Miss Elaine brought us sweet tea and then went back inside to tend to her children.

"What this lady done to upset the Klan?" I asked Erik. " 'Sides exist?"

"Her husband," he said, "not her. He tried to register to vote. Folks might get away with that in Atlanta. But crackers don't tolerate voting Negroes out here."

Crackers didn't tolerate voting Negroes most places. Millen aint have a single registered voter who was colored, far as I'd ever heard. Every now and then, somebody tried, but they were always sent away for one reason or another, and none of them had ever put up a fight about it. Stories of the race riot, passed down, probably had a lot to do with that. Wasn't anybody crazy enough to push it. I thought about the people who'd left Millen, left the South, after the riot. I wondered if they voted, if their children voted, wherever they were now, and what else had changed in their lives because they left.

"You ever think about leaving?" I asked Erik.

"Where? Georgia?"

"The South."

He shook his head. "Naw. I wouldn't make no sense up North. Even less out West. Everything I know right here. All my people here, living and dead both."

"In Miss'ssippi?"

"How you know that?"

"Just guessing." I didn't want to say Dexter told me.

"Where you from?" he asked me.

"Millen, Georgia. You aint never heard of it."

"What it like?"

"Slow. I never knew how slow until I came to Atlanta," I said.

"Every place slow compared to Atlanta, I reckon." He sipped his sweet tea and looked up and down the road. A truck was coming, but he didn't look worried about it. It drove past, and a colored man waved out the window. Erik waved back. I wondered what he looked like naked. I wondered if all the hair on his body was curly like the patch on his chest.

"What you do when you aint on guard duty?" I asked him.

"Work, most of the time."

"Where?"

"I got a night shift at the Royal Peacock. Washing dishes, mostly. Sometime waiting tables if somebody don't show up for work. I get off there 'round four in the morning. Then I go straight to work on the garbage truck."

"When you sleep?"

"Aint never needed too much of that. I always worry 'bout missing something." He took another sip of sweet tea. "You go to school?"

"Naw. My ma been sick, so I been looking after her and Daddy and my brothers. If I go back home, I probably have to get a job. Once Ma get better, I mean."

"*If* you go back?" he asked.

I don't even know why I said that. Unless a whole lot changed in the next day, I aint have anywhere else to go *but* back.

"You thinking 'bout staying here? 'Cause we can use a girl can handle a shotgun."

"How much guard duty pay?"

"Not a penny," he said.

"Mmm-hmm. That's what I thought." I was only joking about guard duty pay, but then I had another thought, a serious one. "What about the Royal Peacock? They hiring down there?"

"Might be. They lose a lot of waitresses on account of all the men grabbing at 'em all night."

That didn't sound like the job for me. "They don't hire girls on the garbage truck, do they?"

"Naw."

I sighed. "Well, how I'm gon' feed and clothe myself if I stay?"

He sucked his teeth. "You could get you a husband in five minutes flat, pretty as you is."

"I aint got plans for no husband," I told him. "I'm working on being a old maid."

He laughed. "Well, we can use a *old maid* can handle a shotgun, even more."

He laughed again, and I laughed with him. Truth was, I liked the idea. I ran my thumb across the butt of the shotgun and imagined myself in Erik's place, standing at the railing, watching the road, a little scared, sure, but still calling the shots, still choosing for myself.

A little after seven, Mr. Greene arrived home from work, ready to look after his family himself, with a rifle, a pistol, and a willing neighbor to help him with the job. Erik said he needed to stop home, to drop off his guns and pick up his uniforms, before taking me back to Mrs. Broussard's and then heading straight off to work.

When we got to his apartment building, we drove past the lot where Dexter and I had parked earlier that day, and pulled up beside the road instead. Erik turned off the engine, but he didn't move to get out the car. He sat there for a moment, before turning to me and saying, "I'd be mighty glad if you did stay in Atlanta," and smiling his bashful smile. Next thing I knew, I'd leaned over and kissed him smack on the mouth. I drew back, shocked at myself, then went on ahead and kissed him again. He slipped his arms around my waist, and we kissed and kissed, there in the car in the fading light.

"I aint see that coming," he said, when we paused to breathe.

I was about to go back in for another round, when out the corner of my eye, I saw a car full of white men drive by, followed by another, and then a third. Erik saw my face and looked where I was looking. We watched a line of cars and trucks, a caravan of ten automobiles full of crackers, drive slowly down the street and stop at the corner.

"What the hell they doing?" Erik asked.

They were just sitting there at the corner, not moving on.

"Let's get out of here," I told him.

He shook his head. "Charlie might be home. I can't just leave. Let's hurry up and get inside."

He got out the car and I did, too. He grabbed my hand, and we hurried up the front steps of the complex, and around the side to the back, out of sight of the street. Erik felt in his pocket, then groaned. "I left my keys in the car! Shit!"

He banged on the back door. Brother Maurice opened it and peeked out.

"Erik? Whatchu doin' knocking on the back door?"

"I aint got my key."

He tried to move inside, but Brother Maurice stood in his way.

"Whatchu doin' here? You supposed to be out at the Greenes'."

"I'm done over there!" Erik told him, sounding mad now. "Nigger, move out the damn way! The Klan out here!"

Maurice frowned. "You can't come in right now. We having a private meeting."

"This my house! Go have a meeting at your own house!"

"You know my mama don't let me have people over!"

Erik pushed the door hard, knocking Brother Maurice back. We hurried inside and then shut the door quick.

"You aint heard what I said about the Klan? Get your gun," Erik said, taking his pistol out of his waistband. I thought about the shotgun we'd left in the trunk.

"I know," Brother Maurice said, calm, like he wasn't worried about it a'tall.

"You *know*?" Erik studied him. "Maurice, what the hell going on?"

"*Brother* Maurice!"

We were standing in the back hallway, and I could see through to the front of the tiny apartment, to the kitchen, where four colored men stood huddled together. They were all in dark suits. The tallest one—a high-yellow Negro with pointy ears and browline glasses—was talking in a low voice to the others. He caught sight of me watching them and frowned. He broke away from the others and walked toward us.

"What's going on back here?" he asked.

"Nothing, sir," Brother Maurice said. "It's just some friends of mine."

The tall man looked at Erik and me, and then back at Brother Maurice again. "This is not a high school dance, Brother. This is serious business here."

There was a knock on the front door, so loud I jumped. What sounded like a white man's voice called out from the other side, "Jeremiah?"

"Yes, sir," came one of the colored men's voices in reply.

The tall man looked tense. "These kids can't be here."

"This my house!" Erik said again.

"Listen, Erik," Brother Maurice told him. "We got big things going on in here that I can't tell you about right now. But I'll fill you in later, I swear. Right now, you got to go in your room and stay in there."

"Nigger—"

"It's for your own safety," the tall man said.

At first, Erik didn't look like he was going to do what they said. But then he let out a long breath. "Yeah. Alright. But you gon' have a whole lot of explaining to do, *Maurice.*"

Erik took my hand and pulled me into a small room.

"I need to get back to Mrs. Broussard's," I said.

"You want to go out there now? With the Klan hanging 'round?"

I shook my head, no. "What they doing here?"

"I wish I knew."

"Who those colored men?"

"Look like Muslims," he said.

"What's that?"

"A religion. Aint too many 'round here, though. Sound like they from up North."

He opened the door a crack. We peeked through and saw a white man standing in the kitchen with the colored men. He looked to be in his forties, short and scrawny, and wearing a hat like nothing I'd never seen before, a fedora with a crown so high it looked like something a witch would have on. Brother Maurice and the four other colored men stood facing him.

"If I'm not out of here in fifteen minutes," he said, looking up at them, "we gonna burn this place to the ground."

"No, sir," one of the colored men said. "Aint no need for all that. You welcome to invite your friends in."

The scrawny man went outside. I glanced at Erik, who looked as confused as me. A minute later, the Klansman came back in with four of his buddies. One of them was wearing a gray suit and tie, but the rest were dressed more casual, in overalls and shirtsleeves.

I reckoned the scrawny one felt more at ease now his friends were in the room, because he took off his hat and they all moved to sit down at the table, where sandwiches, cold drinks, and cookies were laid out.

"Cookies with the Klan," Erik mumbled. "Don't that beat all."

It beat all, sho'nuff. But Erik was standing so close to me I could smell something like cologne under his nervous sweat, and some part of me was thinking about kissing him again.

"The papers got it wrong about the Ku Klux Klan," the scrawny man was saying. "We don't hate all niggers. There *are* some good niggers. I got some working for me. What we don't like is the bad ones. The lazy ones don't want to work. Or the ones want to start trouble 'cause they aint happy just being niggers and letting whites be whites. That's where y'all and us agree. Y'all don't like the bad niggers, either, do you?"

The colored men didn't say anything to that. It was dead quiet in there. After a moment, somebody cleared their throat.

Finally, the man in the browline glasses spoke. "There will inevitably be violence between the races one day, especially if the black man doesn't acquire some land separate from the white man," he said, sounding like he was reading from a book. "The Nation of Islam does not support Jim Crow segregation. Nor do we believe it is the will of Allah for the black man and his enemy, the white man, to live together peacefully. Therefore, we want total, complete separation."

The Klansmen sat listening quietly, nodding here and there. A few of them munched on cookies.

The tall man continued, "The Honorable Elijah Muhammad teaches us that after centuries of slavery, the black man in America is entitled to certain things. One of those things being land. The same land that his ancestors earned with their blood and sweat when they were forced to toil for the white man's benefit. Land, free and clear, that the black man can develop as a separate black nation. The Honorable Elijah Muhammad stands willing to accept the help of any whites who would assist black people in acquiring land for this purpose—let's say a county, for starters—here in Georgia or elsewhere in the Deep South." He took a sip of water. "Let me be crystal clear, so there is no misunderstanding. We want *separation*—not segregation."

The scrawny man looked puzzled. He glanced around at the other Klansmen.

"Your system, *segregation,* exploits black people," the tall man said. "It forces them into complete dependency on whites. The black man has to go to the white man for a job, or a parcel of land to grow crops, or any- and everything else he needs in order to shelter, feed, and clothe his own family. He has no way of striking out on his own. We want a new system. One that is equitable and truly *separate* in every way."

The scrawny white man shrugged. "It's all the same thing to us. Long as you stay over there, we don't care what you call it."

The other Klansmen nodded, agreeing.

The colored leader looked bothered. I could tell he was trying to make them see a distinction they couldn't see, and it vexed him.

"Don't make no difference to them," Erik whispered, more to himself than to me.

I reckoned he was wrong, though. Seemed to me, white folk didn't want colored folk to have nothing of our own, separate or not. Everybody I knew who'd ever left Millen to go up North had to leave at night, because if white people saw them trying to get out, they'd be harassed, or worse. When Daddy's friend Mr. Roland got ready to leave, he went to the train station in Augusta, hoping no white folks would recognize him over there and try to stop him. "They rather kill you than let you get out." White people wanted us near enough that they could work us to death for their profit. If they were keen on separation, it would've happened a long time ago. But they hadn't ever been keen on it. And I didn't think this scrawny Klansman or his friends, who looked like every other poor white trash I'd ever seen, sunburnt red necks and all, was about to change any of it. Only reason to meet with men like this was to negotiate a cross-burning, or maybe some group goat-fornication. Wasn't no way in the world these overall-clad crackers had any say in the handing over of a whole county to colored people, even if they wanted to do it. And these colored men didn't sound any less ridiculous. I'd been around enough Negroes who talked until they put you to sleep about things they had no control over, to know them when I heard them. What county was the likes of *Brother Maurice* fixing to acquire? But I'll tell you what: They all looked dead serious, anyhow. It took a lot of effort not to laugh out loud at how serious they all looked.

We stood there listening for a few more minutes, as they went back and forth about a whole lot of nothing. When one of the colored men said, "One of the counties right outside Atlanta would be good. We don't want nothing too far out," I was through.

"How much longer we gon' stand here listening to this?" I whispered to Erik.

"We can't leave 'fore they do," he said, still peering out. "You seen how many of them was in them cars. It's still a bunch of them outside."

"That don't mean we got to stand here listening at the

door. Aint nothing but a bunch of nonsense. We could do something else."

He looked at me now. "Like what?"

I went and sat on the bed. He closed the door, quiet but quick, and came and sat by me. We started kissing again. Right when it was getting hot and heavy, the voices in the other room got loud.

"We will not participate in any violence against King!"

We stopped kissing.

"They talking about Martin Luther King," I said.

Erik nodded.

Violence was something to take the Klan seriously about. We both moved back to the door, and Erik cracked it open again.

"You told us yourself," the scrawny Klansman was saying. "Violence is needed against bad niggers leading the rest of y'all astray."

"The Nation of Islam will in *no way* assist you in doing physical harm to King," the colored leader said again. "We'll worry about our *own* traitors and hypocrites, and you can worry about yours."

"*You* don't have to kill him!" the Klansman said. "We'll take care of that."

"We will not collude with you to harm Dr. King or any other of our own, in *any* way."

All the men got quiet. Seemed like something might happen. I started to feel scared again. I saw Erik put a hand on his pistol. But then there was the sound of throat-clearing, and they started talking about land again.

I sat back down on the bed, more for comfort now than fooling around, which I'd lost interest in. What they'd said about Reverend King had rattled me. At first, I thought the turning in my stomach was on account of that. But then a queasy feeling ran all over me, and I jumped up.

"Where the outhouse?"

"The head 'cross the hall," Erik said.

I started toward the door, but he stopped me. "You can't hold it?"

"No," I told him. "I need it *now*. 'Less you want me to be sick all over your bedspread."

"We aint supposed to—"

I pushed past him, pulled the door open, and ran out. But it was already too late. The moment I crossed the threshold, a river of hot vomit surged out of me and all over the floor. My stomach churned again, my legs went weak, and I fell to my knees. I put my hand on my stomach and groaned. That's when I heard the sound of pistols being cocked. When I looked up, I saw, through bleary eyes, the Muslims pointing guns at the Klansmen, and the Klansmen pointing guns right back. Erik had his gun out, too, aiming it at one of the Klan. The tall man, the colored leader, was the only one gunless. He had his hands up, moving them in a downward motion, trying to calm the others.

"Now, everybody just hold on," he said. "Just hold on."

"Who the hell is that?" the scrawny Klansman asked, nodding toward Erik. "Wasn't nobody else supposed to be in here."

"He lives here," the tall man said. "They're not here to cause any trouble. It looks like the young lady was trying to get to the toilet."

I felt another wave of queasiness. I needed to get up off the floor and get to the bathroom, but my legs wouldn't work. I retched again, right there with all of them watching me.

"Oh, for God's sake," one of the white men said. I didn't know which one, because I was staring at the floor. I couldn't bear to look up.

I heard water running, and then I felt a hand on my shoulder. It was the colored leader, crouched down next to me. He had a wet handkerchief. He held it out to me. I took it and wiped my mouth.

"Thank you, sir," I said to him.

"Can you stand, sister?" he asked me.

I reckon that last retch did what it needed to, because my legs were working again. With the tall man's help, I stood up.

"This girl's no danger to anyone," he said. "Brothers, lower your weapons."

The Muslims did what he said, but Erik kept his gun right where it was.

"Young brother," the colored leader said. "*Please.*"

Erik slowly lowered his pistol. Once he did, the Klansmen did the same.

"Brother," he said to Erik, "it's time to take this young lady home."

• • •

Back in the car, I couldn't even look at Erik. He kept trying to talk to me—about everything we'd seen and heard—but the most I could do was nod and say things like, "mmm-hmm" and "sho'nuff." I'd never been so embarrassed in my life. But when we drove up to Mrs. Broussard's house, and I saw unfamiliar cars parked in the driveway and along the street in front, I snapped out of it quick.

"I'll walk you to the door," Erik said.

I sat straight up and looked right at him. "No," I told him. "Let's say goodbye here."

I'd figured out what kind of people would be at this party, and much as I liked Erik, I didn't have no reason to think he was somebody safe to bring around those kind of people.

"When you going back home?" he asked me. "*If* you go."

"Sometime tomorrow, I reckon."

"I sure wouldn't mind getting a letter from you," he said. "Erik Johnson. Six hundred Terry Street Southeast. You gon' remember that?"

"I'll remember," I told him.

He leaned over to kiss me. On account of all the retching, I gave him my cheek. It still felt good, his lips on me. I got a tingle all the way down. And I didn't ask Jesus for forgiveness for it, either.

13

When I got in the house, I saw a few guests had arrived but the party wasn't in full swing yet. The people who were there were mostly women—in their thirties, well-dressed—and they were gathered in the living room, with drinks and fancy little bites of things to eat. There were a couple of men, too, including Mr. Locke, who was standing by the bar cart—which had been wheeled in from the dining room—pouring himself a drink. I thought about going right over and asking him about a job. But it felt like that would be putting the cart before the horse. I still needed an abortion, otherwise I couldn't go anywhere, anyhow. But then again, he was like to leave once the party was over, and I wouldn't ever see him again. So, this was my only chance.

"Doris!" Mrs. Lucas appeared, looking scandalized. "Where have you been? I was worried to death."

"I went for a walk," I told her.

"A walk? Where? I drove all around the neighborhood looking for you."

I didn't want to tell her I'd run off with a man. Even if I hadn't asked Jesus for forgiveness, I cared what Mrs. Lucas thought.

"I seen a friend," I said. "We took a drive."

"What friend?"

"His name Erik. He a friend of Mrs. Broussard's nephew. He real nice."

I could tell by the look on her face that she didn't like the idea of me disappearing with some man I'd just met.

"Doris," she said, "I know you're a smart girl and you can look after yourself. But I brought you to Atlanta, and that means that while we're here, you're my responsibility. Please don't go running off without telling me where you're going."

"Yes, ma'am. I'm sorry, Mrs. Lucas. I was so upset, I wasn't thinking."

She sighed. "I know."

"Mrs. Broussard hear anything back?"

"No news yet." She put a hand on my arm. "We'll get it sorted out, sugar. Even if it doesn't happen here. We'll get it all sorted out. Try not to worry."

I glanced over at Mr. Locke again. Mrs. Lucas noticed me noticing him.

"Would you like me to talk to Mr. Locke for you?" she asked.

"No, ma'am," I said. "Thank you, but I think I ought to do it myself."

She made a face like she wasn't sure she liked that idea, and I remembered she'd asked me to stay in my room until the party was over.

"I'll go down to my room soon as I'm done talking to him," I told her.

"Well," she said, "I guess it doesn't matter so much anymore. You already know about Sylvia and . . . well . . ." She looked around at the other guests. "Her friends."

"I can stay, then?"

"Only if you promise to be discreet," she said. "People like us? There aren't a lot of places we can feel safe in this world. If you stay, you can never talk about this party, or anyone you saw here. At least until we're all dead. Understand?"

"Yes, ma'am."

"Well, alright." She patted my arm. "I'm going to get changed. You alright on your own?"

I wondered if I should change, too, then remembered I didn't have much of anything to change into. "I aint got nothing good enough to wear to a fancy party like this."

"I'll see what Sylvia has." I didn't think I could fit anything of Mrs. Broussard's, but Mrs. Lucas said, "She hasn't always been the string bean she is now."

She smiled then and walked off. The second she was gone, I took a deep breath, and without giving myself a moment to change my mind, I went right over to Mr. Locke, who was still standing alone by the bar cart.

"Excuse me, sir? Mr. Locke?"

"Miss Doris. I was wondering where you disappeared to. Come on have a drink with me."

"Oh, I don't . . ."

But he was already pouring a glass of whiskey. He handed it to me and raised his own.

"To the night ahead," he said, with a little twinkle in his eye, and we clinked glasses.

He took a gulp of his drink, and not wanting to be rude, especially since I was fixing to ask him for something, I took a gulp of mine, too. When I tell you I almost choked from the burn in my throat? Even now, I don't like the taste of whiskey. But back then? When I'd never had so much as a sip before? Ooh, chile. But I didn't let on. I smiled and nodded, like downing turpentine was old news to me.

He laughed, tickled. "Best kind of friend in the world is a woman who can hold her liquor!" he said and took another swig.

Now was my chance. *Come on, Doris.*

"Mr. Locke? You think it might be a job for me in your theater company?"

"A job?"

"Yes, sir. I'll take anything. I'm real good at cleaning up after folks. And I can read good."

"How good?"

"Real good," I told him.

He nodded. "That's a point in your favor, sho'nuff. The leads do like to run lines with their maids if they can."

"The leads?"

"The lead actors and actresses," he said. "Come to think of it, I do believe Pauli's looking for a new girl."

"Pauli?"

"Pauli McDaniel. Our *star.*"

"Oh, yes, sir. That's right. Pauli McDaniel. I 'member now."

He laughed. "You don't know anything about the company you're trying to work for, do you?"

"No, sir," I admitted. "But I can learn fast."

"I didn't know anything about Licorice when I came on, either. I was just trying to get the hell away from Wrens."

"Wrens? You from Wrens, sir?" Wrens wasn't but two towns over from Millen.

"You know it?" he asked.

"I got kin there."

"What's the name?"

"Wadley."

"I know some Wadleys! Chester and . . . Bernice?"

"Bernadine."

"Those your people?" he asked, excited.

"Yes, sir," I said, excited, too.

"I used to pick cotton right alongside Chester and his brother. They always helped me when I fell behind. They're good, hardworking people, no doubt about that." He chuckled and put his arm around my shoulders like we were peas in a pod, me and him, and said, "Pauli'll be through here tonight. I can't promise she'll hire you, of course—that's her call since she'd be the one paying you. But I'll introduce you and put in a good word."

"Thank you, Mr. Locke," I said.

He laughed. "Hold on to that thank you until you get the job."

• • •

When I went to my room to get changed for the party, I found a dress laid out on the bed. I held it up. It was a swing dress, sky blue with a thin white trim around the collar and along the hem. The material was lightweight and summery. The dress looked the right size, which surprised me because Mrs. Broussard was small-chested, and this dress had space for an ample bosom. That was lucky for me, since my bosom had started out ample, and was only getting ampler by the day.

I washed up and changed into the dress, careful not to muss my new hairdo. I stood in front of the mirror. My cheeks were fuller than usual, owing to the pregnancy. That, plus the new hair and the dress, made it almost like a different person was looking back at me. I wanted my cheekbones back to normal. But the rest of it, I liked. And not just the hair and the dress, either. I felt like a different person inside, too, and I liked that. I felt myself opening up to the world. I had so many questions—about theater and sex and Negroes living in France. I could feel these questions buzzing in my brain, and moving through me, tingling in my fingertips. I couldn't wait to get back to the party.

When I got upstairs, I saw many more guests had come. Voices mingled with music from the record player—Brook Benton singing "Kiddio"—and laughter, and sometimes the sound of glasses clinking. Mrs. Broussard was in the living room, sitting on the sofa, with her hand on some woman's thigh. The old me would've turned right around and hightailed it back to my room. And, truth be told, I did think about Pastor Mills and roaring lions and what-all. But 1 Peter didn't seem that interesting to me anymore.

Mrs. Lucas had said she thought Mrs. Broussard was lonely. But she didn't look lonely to me, sitting there laughing at something Mr. Locke was saying, smacking him on the arm with the hand that wasn't squeezing the thigh of a woman who looked ten years too young for her. I wanted to know who this younger woman was. But the last time I'd spoken to Mrs. Broussard, I'd called her a liar, so I couldn't rightly plop down next to them and start asking questions. Instead, I stood there near the doorway, watching them all.

On the other side of Mr. Locke was another man, an older man with fuzzy graying hair and glasses, who was laughing along with them. Next to him, in an armchair, sat Mrs. Lucas, who was talking to someone I thought was a man from behind, but once I got a better look turned out to be a pretty woman dressed up in a man's clothes. The woman was sitting on the arm of the chair, leaning down close to Mrs. Lucas, talking soft and grinning at her, and I could tell from the way Mrs. Lucas sat with her body turned toward the woman that she liked it plenty. After a couple of minutes, the woman got up and went to the bar cart. Quick as a flash, a different woman—also pretty, but wearing a dress—came and sat down on the arm of Mrs. Lucas's chair and whispered something in her ear. Mrs. Lucas smiled and touched the woman's arm.

I wondered where Julia Avery was, and no sooner than I thought it, she bust through the door, talking about, "I'm here, y'all! Where the booze at?" and everybody fell out, laughing and screaming with excitement. Pearl came out of nowhere to take her coat, then disappeared as quick as she'd showed up. Mrs. Broussard gave Julia a big hug.

"Julia, I'm so pleased you made it."

"I almost didn't," she said. "Traffic was horrendous downtown. Took me twice as long to get here as it ought to."

"Probably that student conference," Mrs. Broussard said, frowning.

"Cate!" Julia said when she saw Mrs. Lucas, and kissed her on both cheeks. I looked around for the woman Mrs. Lucas had been talking to, but she was gone.

The man with gray hair and glasses got up off the sofa and offered his seat to Miss Julia.

"Bayard!" she said. "I didn't know you were in town!"

"Nobody knows," he said. "So don't tell nobody if they ask."

Pearl appeared again, holding out a drink to Miss Julia. She looked surprised as she took it. "Well, that was fast. Thank you, Pearl," she said. Then, to Mrs. Broussard, "The service here sure is top-notch, Syl."

Mrs. Broussard looked pleased. "Pearl's a gem. I've always been blessed with a knack for finding good help."

"I'm still getting used to *having* help," Miss Julia said. "Even after all these years. I've never liked strange people in my private space. I didn't grow up siddity like you and Cate. That's the thing you never liked about me, right, Syl?"

"That's not true, Julia," Mrs. Broussard said. "You know there's lots of things I never liked about you." And everybody fell out again. Over in the corner, I laughed, too. I wasn't sure if those two loved or hated each other, but it was entertaining, right on.

I saw Mr. Locke introduce himself to Miss Julia, and then Mrs. Broussard's younger friend did the same. Mrs. Broussard noticed me standing there watching it all, and locked eyes with me for a moment, before turning to greet some friends who'd just arrived. I looked down at the floor, feeling ashamed of myself. What was I thinking, sassing a woman in her own house, then showing up to her party, wearing her dress? Lord knows Ma raised me better than that. I wished I could melt into the wall. I thought about going back to my room, hiding out until the party was over, and then finding Mrs. Broussard later and apologizing. But when I looked up, she was standing in front of me.

"Doris, I want to apologize," she said, "for not telling you sooner about the doctor. And for saying what I said about Catie and me. I shouldn't have. It was reckless. And it wasn't fair to Catie, or to you. No one wants to carry a secret they never asked to be told in the first place."

I stared at her. Honest to God, I aint know what to say. I wasn't used to grown folks saying they were sorry. "It's . . . it's alright, Mrs. Broussard."

"You won't ever tell, will you?"

"No, ma'am."

She smiled at me.

"Who's this sweet young thing?" asked the woman whose thigh Mrs. Broussard had been holding on to earlier, appearing at her side with a fresh drink.

"Catie's niece," Mrs. Broussard said, taking the glass. "Doris."

"Well, hello, Catie's-niece-Doris," the woman said. "I'm Ruth."

Ruth looked to be about twenty-five, with creamy coffee-colored skin, a gap between her two front teeth, and bright eyes.

"Evening, ma'am."

She looked me up and down, her eyes widening, then pointed at me with a pink-polished fingertip. "I believe I have that very same dress!"

"That *is* your dress," Mrs. Broussard said to her. "I loaned it to Doris for the party."

Finally, the dress's measurements made sense.

"Oh! Well, I guess I must've left it on Sylvia's floor one day while I was visiting," Ruth said, and winked at me. "The only question is, what the hell did I wear home?" She cackled, bending forward at the waist and slapping me on the arm.

Mrs. Broussard smiled and shook her head.

Ruth sipped her drink, then looked me over again and asked, "How old are you, Catie's-niece-Doris?"

"Not old enough," Mrs. Broussard said, "so, calm yourself down."

"Oh, don't be such a prude, Sylvia, I'm only messing. Tell me something, honey. You like girls?"

"No, ma'am. Not *that way*."

"Well, why the hell not?" She waved a hand at me. "You don't know what you're missing." She walked off without another word.

Mrs. Broussard didn't see her go. She was watching Mrs. Lucas and Julia Avery, who were sitting together now, deep in conversation. When she noticed me noticing, she looked embarrassed for a moment, then shrugged and said, "I'm not jealous, if that's what you're thinking."

"No, ma'am, I wasn't thinking that." But I was.

"I know everyone thinks I am, but I'm not. I invited Julia, for goodness' sake. If I'm possessive, it's only of Catie's friendship. But Catie and Julia are not friends, so I've got no reason to be jealous."

"They aint?" I asked.

"Of course not," she said, like it was a dumb question. "It's Julia's fault Catie left Atlanta, and everything and everyone she knew. A friend would've tried to stop her."

So, it wasn't jealousy, after all, but resentment. Mrs. Broussard blamed Miss Julia for losing Mrs. Lucas to Millen.

"Anyhow," she said with a shrug, throwing it off, "now that *you and I* are friends again, there's no need to be over here lurking in the corner. Come on join the party."

The party had grown from just a handful of women to two dozen of them, dancing and talking and drinking. I wondered if they were all inverts and, if they were, how Mrs. Broussard had met so many. Some of them looked like they went together, holding hands and dancing close, and some didn't. There were women in their twenties, thirties, forties, fifties, and one woman looked sixty-five if she was a day. Every one of them was dressed like she had money. Julia Avery wasn't the only one wearing a diamond, by far. And they all looked like they just got their hair done.

Mrs. Broussard took my arm and led me over to the sofa, sat me down next to Ruth, and went off to mingle with her other guests. Ruth was talking to Mr. Bayard.

"You in town for the sit-ins?" she was asking him.

"Don't say it too loud," he told her, putting his finger to his lips. "I'm here in my capacity as mentor to many of the Snick youth, but unofficially. I don't want to be the cause of any tension between them and SCLC. Any more than there already is, of course."

"Why would it be a problem?" Mrs. Lucas asked.

"The SCLC leadership is a little skittish right now about being associated with the likes of me," he said.

"The likes of you, the likes of all of us here, got every right to be part of the movement," said Mr. Locke, sounding angry.

"Go on and tell 'em, Carlton," Miss Julia said. "Because I, for one, am sick to death of Negroes and their narrow-ass ideas of freedom that don't include nobody that don't think and act exactly like they do. I've always admired you," she told Mr. Bayard, "living your life out in the open, and fuck 'em if they don't like it."

"I appreciate you, Julia," Mr. Bayard said. "But it's precisely because I'm open about it, because I declare homosexuality, that I'm a liability to the movement, as far as some people are concerned. To Martin's credit, he's never been one of those people. Well, until now."

"What changed?" Miss Julia asked.

"Well, *certain politicians* didn't want SCLC organizing a protest at the DNC last summer and upsetting the white folks."

"A certain politician rhymes with *foul*?"

Mr. Bayard laughed. "Yeah, that's the one. He said if we didn't cancel it, he was going to start a rumor that Martin and I are lovers."

"He did not!" Ruth shouted.

"Oh, he did."

"Is that why you left SCLC?" Mrs. Lucas asked.

He nodded, looking pained.

"But that's *ridiculous,*" said Miss Julia. "Who would ever believe such a thing?"

Mr. Bayard nodded again. "That's what I said. But Martin didn't want to take the chance."

"Well, fuck him!"

Mr. Bayard chuckled. "That's your own cousin you're talking about."

"By marriage."

"Oh, stop it," said Mrs. Lucas. "You love Martin."

"I do love him," Miss Julia admitted. "But he's always been too concerned with his image. If threatening to start a rumor about who Martin goes to bed with is all a man like Adam Clayton Powell has to do to get his way, to the detriment of the entire cause, something aint right." She shook her head. "*Lovers*. Please. Martin should be so lucky to land a man like you, short as he is." She was already laughing before she finished the sentence, and everybody else was, too. Mr. Locke almost choked on his drink. Mr. Bayard near-bout fell out his chair. Mrs. Lucas laughed so hard tears came into her eyes.

"If anybody tells Corey I said that, I'll call you a damn liar!" Miss Julia said, through her own tears, and they all laughed even harder.

When the hooting and hollering died down, Mr. Bayard said, "I'll tell you what, though: The next generation, the ones coming up now, are different. They don't care about gay or straight, men or women, none of that. Snick got more girls running the show than men."

I thought about what Ruby Doris and Diane had said about men taking all the credit at SNCC. And I remembered how disgusted Dexter had been about James Baldwin and his book. So I doubted what Mr. Bayard said was true. I wasn't the only one, either. Mr. Locke shook his head. "I don't know about all that, Bayard."

"Well, we got one of the youth right here," Ruth said, placing her hands on my shoulders, "so, let's ask her. What do you think about homosexuals leading the cause, Catie's-niece-Doris?"

"How do you know she aint one of us?" Miss Julia wanted to know.

"I asked her," said Ruth.

"Of course you did," said Mr. Locke, with a chuckle.

"Well, then?" Ruth asked, looking at me.

"You don't have to answer that, Doris," Mrs. Lucas told me.

"Sure she does," Ruth said. She was smiling, good-natured, but her eyes looked plenty serious. It made me uneasy, being put on the spot like that, and I wondered who raised her to be so rude. It was years before I understood that the look I saw in her eyes was fear. I might've been the only one there who wasn't "that way," and that meant everyone else there had to trust me. Ruth wanted me to prove I was worthy of that trust.

But Mrs. Lucas wasn't having any of it. "Let her be," she

said, in the same tone she sometimes used in class, when Marvin or one of the others needed to be brought in line quick. And just like Marvin and them, Ruth did what she said. She released my shoulders and shrugged. "Fine. Never mind, then."

"That's cheating, anyhow," Mr. Locke said. "We already know what Miss Doris thinks. Nobody comes to a party at Sylvia's, when Alonzo's out of town, who got a problem with homosexuals!"

I was relieved not to have had to answer. Truth was, I wasn't sure what I thought. Hating homosexuals didn't seem right. It never had, and did even less now that I'd met some. I didn't have a problem with any of these people being part of the movement, or even leading it. But I didn't see why expecting them to keep their personal business to themselves was so much to ask. I didn't see why Mr. Bayard had to "declare" it. It seemed tacky to me, to flaunt it that way. But I wasn't dumb enough to say any of that in this company, so I just laughed along and kept it to myself.

A Chuck Berry album was spinning on the record player, and when the last song ended, Mrs. Broussard put on Dinah Washington and Brook Benton singing, "A Rockin' Good Way." The first woman Mrs. Lucas had been talking to earlier came over.

"Come dance with me, Cate," she said, holding out her hand. Up close, she was more than pretty. She had smooth dark skin, dramatic, heavy-lidded eyes, and the smile she flashed made me want to dance with her.

Mrs. Lucas took her hand and they moved to where furniture had been pushed back to make space for dancing. Mrs. Lucas put her hands on the woman's shoulders, while the woman slipped her arms around Mrs. Lucas's waist, and they swayed together in rhythm with the song.

Miss Julia watched them. Thick smoke from her cigarette shielded her face for a few moments, and when it cleared away, I could see she didn't look happy. Mrs. Broussard noticed, too. "I bet that doesn't happen a lot, does it, Julia?" she asked. "Having a woman snatched from the all-consuming glow of your attention?"

Miss Julia cut her eyes at Mrs. Broussard. "Don't be a bitch, Sylvia."

Ruth looked annoyed. "Can *we* please dance, Syl?" she asked. "Or y'all fixing to bore me to death shit-talking each other over Cate?"

Mrs. Broussard and Ruth went to dance. I watched Ruth slip her arms around Mrs. Broussard's waist and pull her close, whispering something in her ear, and damn if Mrs. Broussard didn't giggle like a schoolgirl.

A woman appeared and asked Miss Julia to cut a rug with her. Miss Julia smiled. "Thanks, darlin', but I was just on my way to get some air." She stood up. "Come on, keep me company," she said. She was looking at me, but I couldn't believe I was the one she was talking to. I glanced around. "Me?"

She gave me a look like she thought I might be dim-witted. "Yes, you, darlin'. I'm looking right at you, aint I?"

14

The air out on the sleeping porch was cool and smelled like rain. It was about nine o'clock, and the sky was cloudy and purple. I sat down on a rocker while Miss Julia stood beside an open window and lit a cigarette.

"I realized I never answered the question you asked me earlier today," she said to me. "About my favorite place. You still interested?"

"Oh, yes," I told her. "Mighty interested."

"Well, if you mean abroad, Amsterdam's a really good time. And Berlin, too. But for me, there's still nowhere like Memphis. Or Harlem, especially on a Saturday night. And if I'm forced to choose one favorite, it'll be Atlanta every time."

That surprised me. Sure, Atlanta was the most exciting place *I'd* ever been. But I hadn't ever been nowhere. "Why?" I asked her.

"Atlanta saved me," she said. "It still saves me, whenever I need it to. Growing up, Atlanta was a beacon to me. I thought if I could just get here, that would be enough. But that felt like a tall order because hardly anybody I knew ever left Alabama. My mama had ten children. Her mama had fourteen before her. Where were they going with all those damn kids?" She shook her head. "Still, I knew I wouldn't survive there. Some parts of me would, sure. But the things that make me the most myself? Those parts would dry up, like dead leaves, and get crushed under somebody's foot. I was about seven or eight when I understood that. From then on, I looked for any chance to get out. I could sing, but I knew singing wasn't going to be the way out, so I focused on my schooling.

"I was nineteen when I got a scholarship to Spelman. That's when I met the love of my life."

"Aunt Cate?"

She looked at me, surprised. "No, darlin'. Atlanta."

My cheeks burned with embarrassment. I decided to shut up and just listen.

"Once I was here," she said, "singing my way through life didn't seem so impossible. I studied voice and sang in juke joints on the weekends. I started drawing crowds. Juke joints turned into club gigs in Sweet Auburn and, well, maybe you know the rest."

"Yes, ma'am. Yes, Miss Julia."

"Nobody ever believes me when I say this, but I never wanted to be famous. I just wanted to get the hell out of Heiberger. The idea of staying there, waking up next to some man all my life . . . I couldn't bear the thought." She shrugged. "But I suppose if you like boys, that kind of life doesn't seem quite so bad."

"Liking boys don't mean I want to wake up next to one

every day," I told her. "And even if I did want that, it don't mean that's all I want."

"What *do* you want?" she asked me. "To travel? Is that why you were asking about Paris?"

"Maybe so."

"You don't sound at all sure," she said.

"It'd be nice to see some of the world, I reckon. Or maybe I'd be satisfied just to wake up next to myself every morning. And lie there with my own thoughts long as I like. I don't know."

"Sounds like what you want is more choices."

"Yes, ma'am." Then I thought of something. "Do you need any help? On the road? Or in Memphis? I'm a hard worker. And dependable. I'd do a good job for you. I'd do whatever you need."

"Child, I already got more help than I want," she said. "But I'll keep you in mind if anything comes up, alright?"

"Yes, Miss Julia. Thank you."

"Any more questions?"

"Oh, lots."

She laughed. I could tell she liked me. It felt good to be liked by her. "Well, go on," she said. "Ask."

"Are you in love with Aunt Cate?"

Her smile disappeared. She peered at me. "*Who are you?*"

"I . . . told you—"

"Cate doesn't have a niece," she said. "Four nephews: Joshua, Joseph, Julian, and Nestor."

"I'm . . . by marriage," I stammered. "I'm Uncle Robert's niece."

She shook her head. "If you were Robert's niece, Sylvia would've said that. She's funny that way about kin."

I remembered Mrs. Broussard calling Dexter her "step-nephew" and I gave up. What else could I say?

"You one of her students?" she asked me.

I didn't answer.

"Why'd she bring you here?"

I just sat there, not saying shit.

Miss Julia threw her hands up, looking vexed. "You playing deaf and dumb all of a sudden? You not gonna answer my questions at all?"

"All due respect, ma'am," I said, "but you didn't answer mine."

She looked struck, like she couldn't believe I had the gall. Then a grin spread across her face. "Well, shit. You aint near as much of a bumpkin as you put on. You got some wits about you, sho'nuff. Okay, dimples." She pulled a long drag off her cigarette, slow, and blew it out even slower. Then she said, "Sure, I love her. Everyone loves her."

"No, I mean—"

"I know what you mean. And it's like I said. Half the women here are in love with Cate. Or aint you been paying attention?"

Back in Millen, I'd thought of Mrs. Lucas as attractive, but not sexy. She was clever, interesting to talk to, and curious. Those things didn't add up to *desirable,* either in the way I'd been taught to think of it, or in the way men and boys behaved around her. But in this place, among these women, she sure did seem to have what it took.

"Don't tell me Cate has you thinking *I'm* the heartbreaker," Miss Julia said. "She left me."

"Maybe she aint know you loved her," I said, then thought maybe I was saying too much.

Miss Julia shook her head. "She knew I loved her. Trouble was, she wanted me to love *only* her. Cate is an incredible woman, maybe the best person I know. But some of her ideas about love are limited. Like most people's."

"What's so wrong about wanting to feel like somebody loves you the most?"

"*The most?*" She shook her head. "Why should love be a competition?"

I thought I understood what she was saying. And, I thought, if all things were possible, why should Miss Julia love *only* Mrs. Lucas? Why should Mrs. Lucas only be capable of loving Miss Julia if Miss Julia didn't love anybody else? On the other hand, it seemed natural to want to know you were special to somebody, especially if that somebody was special to you.

"Alright," Miss Julia said then. "I answered. Now, it's your turn. Spill it, dimples. Why'd Cate bring you here?"

I couldn't answer the question. I'd promised Mrs. Lucas I'd never tell anyone, and I wasn't about to break my word.

"Answer one more thing for me first," I told her.

She sighed like she was getting annoyed, but said, "Alright, go ahead."

"What do women do in bed together?"

If she looked struck before, she looked ready to hit the floor now.

"My friend Lena said one woman acts like the man, but—"

"Stop!" she shouted, putting up her hands. "Lord! What is this 'acts like the man' nonsense?"

"Well, I—"

"Tell me something, darlin'," she said. "If you see two women sitting around having a conversation, do you imagine one of them is talking like the man?"

I shook my head. "No, ma'am. No, Miss Julia."

"And if you see two women baking a damn pie together, do you think one of them is mixing in the flour like the man?"

"No."

"Of course you don't. So why would one of them be acting 'like the man' in the bedroom? No one 'acts like the man' because there is no man. Whatever they do together, they do it as women. Understand?"

"Yes, Miss Julia."

She nodded, satisfied, then softened. "Far as what they do," she said, "they do whatever they like. Whatever gives them pleasure. Some women like to use their hands, their mouths—"

"Like kissing?"

She peered at me. "Lord, child. How old are you?"

"Seventeen."

"*Seventeen?* And you don't know anything about . . ." Her voice trailed off as she stared at me in disbelief.

Despite my condition, I didn't know much about sex. I was familiar with the kind that involved a boy, a girl, and the missionary position. And, thanks to Genesis, I knew about sodomy. "I spend a lot of time in church," I told Miss Julia.

"Well, that'll do it. There's nothing better for keeping you ignorant about sex than spending a lot of time in church." She rolled her eyes. "I'm talking about going down on each other? Oral sex?"

I knew what oral sex was, but I thought of it as something very nasty women did to very drunk men, and only for money, like when my uncle Al got caught by his wife getting head in a whorehouse, and was left on the spot. I'd never heard of women doing that to each other, and just the notion of it left my bottom lip hanging and my cheeks burning red. I couldn't see no way Jesus could possibly approve of such a thing.

"You alright, darlin'?" Miss Julia asked me.

"Yes, ma'am. I think so."

"I think that's enough sex education for now," she said.

I nodded. Swallowed. "Yes, ma'am. I think so."

She lit another cigarette, then stared at me, eyebrows raised, waiting.

"I can't tell you why I'm here," I said. "I promised I wouldn't tell nobody."

"You little cheat!" she said, pointing a bejeweled finger at me. "And here I was thinking we were building trust between us!"

"I'm real sorry, Miss Julia."

She frowned hard at me for a long moment, then waved her hand. "Fine, don't tell me. Truth is, I like you more for it. I always say it's good to have friends who can keep secrets."

"We friends?" I asked her.

She smiled. "We must be. Sylvia thinks Cate's the reason I came tonight, but she's wrong. As usual. I came for you."

"Ma'am?"

"I been thinking about the other question you asked me," she said. "About how I knew my life could be different. What I told you, about a voice inside me, that's true. But there's another true thing. *I didn't know.* Because nobody can know that. Certainly nobody like us." She took a long drag off her cigarette. "The most true thing is that I made a choice. I chose not to believe all the people who told me my life couldn't be different. And then I kept on choosing. I chose to get on a train. I chose to sing when nobody was paying me a dime to do it. I chose to be brave sometimes, and sometimes I chose to run away scared. Being a colored woman, it's easy to think we don't have many choices, and that's a fact a lot of the time. Too much of the time. But there are so many things we can choose. Maybe they seem like small things and maybe they are. But they add up. If you're lucky, they add up to a life. You hear?"

"Yes, Miss Julia."

"Alright."

When we got back to the party, the music had changed to Chubby Checker, and everybody was up dancing the Twist. Miss Julia poured herself a drink, and I grabbed a Coke from a bucket full of ice that Pearl had put on the bar, and we sat watching for a little while. Mr. Locke was real good at the Twist. He looked just like Chubby doing it on *American Bandstand,* which I'd watched at Lena's house that summer. When the song ended, somebody flipped the record to the other side, and in the few seconds' pause, some people quit dancing, including Mr. Locke, Mr. Bayard, Miss Ruth, and Mrs. Broussard, who all headed for the bar cart. When Mrs. Broussard saw Miss Julia, she frowned, and said, "You been sitting over here all this time? I can't believe it. The famous Julia Avery reduced to a wallflower by the likes of Pauli McDaniel?"

Pauli McDaniel?

"For your information," Miss Julia said, "I've been having a nice conversation with Doris here. And whether I sit or dance has got nothing to do with Pauli or anybody else. Cate is a grown woman, Sylvia. She's perfectly capable of making her own decisions."

"That sounds a lot like what you said when she told you she was going to marry Robert."

Miss Julia got very quiet.

"Lay off her, Syl," Mr. Bayard said.

But she didn't lay off. "Well, it's true. So, why shouldn't I say it?"

"There's plenty true things we shouldn't say," Miss Julia told her, standing up. "I'll give you an example: At least Cate loved Robert. You never wanted a man a day in your life, but you married Alonzo so your folks wouldn't figure out you were one of us deviants. And now you're stuck out here in this house, raising children *he* wanted, while he works late every night and spends a whole lot of weekends out of town—"

"Julia," Mr. Bayard cut in, putting a hand on her arm. "Don't."

"Don't what? We're saying the truth, aren't we?"

I wished she'd stop, too. I felt bad for Mrs. Broussard. Sure, she'd started it. She'd been giving Miss Julia grief all evening. But it seemed like Miss Julia was going for blood.

She took a step closer to Mrs. Broussard. "You tell yourself you lucked out, because Alonzo lets you have your little parties, and your little flings, as long as you're discreet, as long as it doesn't interfere with his business and his reputation, and as long as you keep putting out once or twice a month. But the *truth* is you're a miserable bitch. Which is fine. I mean, everybody's got to be *something*. But I'd rather you didn't take it out on me."

Mrs. Broussard, who'd stood there calm the whole time, sighed and said, easy as you please, "I'm not taking anything out on you, Julia," and ignored the rest of it. She was lying, of course. She was taking Mrs. Lucas's absence out on Miss Julia. But I realized what a tough cookie Mrs. Broussard was. Most people would've been ready to fight or break down in tears after getting told off that bad. "I'm only trying to help," she said.

"I don't need your help," Miss Julia told her.

"Fine." Mrs. Broussard walked off.

Miss Julia looked mad. The vein in her forehead bulged so big I worried it was going to pop. But I was also distracted by the mention of Pauli McDaniel.

The music stopped. Everybody who hadn't already quit dancing, quit then, including Mrs. Lucas and her dancing partner, who came right over to me.

"Doris, this is Pauli McDaniel," Mrs. Lucas said. "She's a player in the Licorice Theater Company."

It was the woman who'd been flirting with Mrs. Lucas the whole night, the pretty one wearing a man's suit.

"Cate says you might be interested in a job," she said.

"Just how many people you got working this job angle for you, Miss Doris?" Mr. Locke asked, then chuckled good-naturedly and downed his drink.

"Oh," I said. "Yes, ma'am, I'm interested in a job."

"I guess you got experience cleaning up after folks?" she asked me.

"Yes, ma'am, plenty."

"I bet you do. What poor colored girl don't?" She looked me up and down again, slowly, then nodded. "If Cate says you alright, you must be. You want the gig, you got it."

I just stared at her, blinking. Then I looked at Mrs. Lucas. She raised her eyebrows at me, as if to say, *Is this what you want?*

"We hit the road again in two weeks," Mr. Locke said.

"But I need you to meet me here in Atlanta a couple days early," Pauli said, "so we can go over the schedule, and I can train you on how I like things. My last girl kept buying me the wrong soap. Had me smelling like lavender a mile away. How hard you think it is to remember what kind of soap to buy?"

"Not hard," I told her. "I'm sure I can do it, ma'am."

"Alright, then."

Suddenly, the music started up again. "Come Rain or Come Shine," the new Ray Charles one. I recognized it from the night before, when Dexter played it for me. I remembered, too, what Mrs. Lucas told me, about the time Miss Julia had sung it onstage, just for her. I thought it was all coincidence, but when I looked, I saw Mrs. Broussard standing at the record player. She'd chosen the song.

People started getting up again to dance, but they didn't rush like before, they drifted, pulled by the slowness of the melody. Almost like it was happening in slow motion, I saw Pauli reaching out for Mrs. Lucas's hand, in the same moment that Mrs. Lucas and Miss Julia turned toward each other. Miss Julia whispered something in Mrs. Lucas's ear, and took her other hand, and they went off together to dance. Mrs. Lucas never even noticed Pauli. Pauli didn't seem to mind too much, though. She winked at me and said, "Don't count me out just yet."

I watched them all dancing, women swaying to Ray Charles's raspy tones, dark and medium-brown and high-yellow arms wrapped around shoulders and waists, eyes so full of desire, and I sure felt God in that house. A more interesting God than I'd ever known.

When the song ended, I watched wide-eyed as Miss Julia leaned in to kiss Mrs. Lucas. But she turned and walked away. I reckoned she was trying not to get "caught up" and I couldn't blame her. Their love seemed like a lot to handle.

I wanted to ask Mrs. Broussard why she'd played the song. She was the only other person who knew what it meant to them—Mrs. Lucas had told me so. And I knew she'd been trying get Miss Julia to dance with Mrs. Lucas. I didn't understand why, especially after the harsh things Miss Julia had said to her. But Mrs. Broussard was nowhere in sight.

After Mrs. Lucas walked away, Miss Julia and Mr. Bayard danced together. I watched them, and the others, for a while, until I felt tired. The clock on the wall said ten twenty-five but it seemed later. I decided that even though nobody had got skunk-drunk and howled naked at the moon, I'd still got more than I could've hoped for out of this party, and I should quit while I was ahead.

15

In my room, I lay on the bed, staring up at the ceiling, thinking about what just happened. I was going on the road with Licorice. It was only a maid's job, but it felt like a miracle. No one in my family ever left Millen for good unless they were run out in the middle of the night. I could leave with Pauli and them on a train in broad daylight. I closed my eyes and felt myself drifting to sleep. I hoped Mrs. Broussard would find another doctor by morning.

About an hour later, I woke up to the sound of knocking. At first, I thought somebody was knocking on my door, but when I realized the sound was coming from farther away, I turned over, determined to sleep through it, whatever it was. But the knocking kept on, and I couldn't settle again on account of it. Then I heard voices in the hallway, too muffled to make out, and I got up.

I opened the door and peeked out. I saw Mrs. Lucas, standing with her back to her own door, which was shut behind her, and Miss Julia, who must've been doing all that knocking, facing her. Mrs. Lucas looked disheveled, her dress off one shoulder, her hair mussed. She was looking at Miss Julia with a stern face. I couldn't hear what Miss Julia was saying, or Mrs. Lucas's reply, because they were both whispering, but the whole thing felt tense. At first. But then, as I stood there watching, Mrs. Lucas seemed to soften. Her shoulders relaxed. Her face went from *no* to *maybe so*. Miss Julia reached out and touched her cheek. She leaned closer, and this time Mrs. Lucas didn't walk away. They kissed, tender at first, and then with more and more passion, so much I was sure they'd burst into flames. But that didn't happen because they stopped when the bedroom door opened and Pauli came out, looking disheveled her own self.

"Well, damn," she said, loud enough that I heard it.

Mrs. Lucas said something in a soft voice, looking real sorry, but I didn't think Pauli was buying it, the way she was shaking her head. Finally, Pauli walked off quick down the hallway. I ducked back inside so she wouldn't see me. After a moment, I peeked back out, just in time to see Mrs. Lucas pull Miss Julia into her room and shut the door.

I knew good and well what I should've done then. I should've closed the door and gone on back to bed. I know that now, and I knew that then. But, Jesus forgive me, that *aint* what I did. What I *did* was tiptoed out into the hallway, got down on my knees in front of the closed door, and peeked through the keyhole. I saw them kissing. I saw them taking each other's clothes off. That's when I knew for sure that if I didn't stop watching, the Good Lord might strike me down, and rightly so.

So, I prayed to Jesus for forgiveness before watching a little bit more. When they'd both got down to their underwear, I tiptoed back to my room.

I was too awake now to even try to sleep. There was a throbbing between my legs. Out of nowhere, I thought about Erik, the hairs peeking out of his shirt and his lips on mine, the way his hands had gripped me, and the throbbing only got worse.

I'd never touched myself in a sinful way, except for when I was a small child and didn't know better. Whenever I got so hot and bothered thinking about some boy that I was tempted to know myself that way, I opened my Bible at the beginning, and let all the begats settle me down. I looked around for my Bible now, but I couldn't find it. I thought, even if Mrs. Broussard was a heathen, there must be a Bible somewhere, even if it was just for mocking. Pearl seemed like the type to carry a small Bible in her pocketbook, on hand to deliver the Word at any moment. But it didn't seem right to disturb her while she was working so hard at the party. So, what could I do? I reckoned if Jesus wanted me to have a Bible in this moment, he would've provided one. And, following that way of thinking, if he hadn't wanted me to touch myself in a sinful way, he would've made me a stronger person. Or at least not thrown all this sex up in front of my face. Maybe he *wanted* me to do it.

I lay back on the bed and was fixing to hike up my nightgown, when I heard another knock. I jumped up faster than a deacon catching the Holy Spirit. Dexter waved at me through the window. The sight of him put a stop to the throbbing. I reckoned Jesus hadn't wanted me to do it after all.

Dexter gestured for me to open the window. I composed myself, made sure the door was locked, then let him in.

"What you doing here again?" I asked, as he climbed in. "You forget another wallet?"

"I'm on my way to a party," he said. "You want to come with me?"

"I just left a party," I told him.

He sucked his teeth. "This aint no party worth being at."

"Why not?" I asked, feeling nervous. Pearl had closed all the curtains, but maybe he saw something.

"It's nothing but old people," he said.

"How you know that?"

"Auntie Sylvia doesn't know anybody younger than thirty," he said. "All her friends are married, and dull as rocks."

I was relieved. But I worried that if I didn't go with him now, he might stick around and see something.

"Alright," I told him. "Let me get my clothes back on and I'll come with you." I moved toward the bathroom. "Stay right here. Don't go nowhere."

16

The party Dexter wanted to take me to was at a restaurant on the edge of downtown, not far from the church where the conference was taking place. On the conference agenda Dexter had given me, it was listed as a "reception." But when we arrived, around eleven at night, it sure looked like a party. People, mostly colored, filled the space. Aretha Franklin's voice spilled out from big black speakers set against a wall. People were dancing, or huddled together laughing, or singing along to the music. This crowd wasn't anything like the one at Mrs. Broussard's. These were mostly young people, and their energy was more hyper. I spotted one of the girls I'd followed into the bathroom earlier, the one called Ruby Doris, dancing the Hully Gully. She looked tired; her shoulders were shaking but her hips barely moved. All Hully, no Gully. I reckoned putting on a conference must be a lot of work, especially if you aint even getting any credit for it. But she was smiling—tired, sho'nuff, but maybe happy, too. Looking around, seemed like everybody was in good spirits, arms and hips and backsides shaking everywhere. Some people danced in groups, but most were paired up. Watching all the couples with their arms wrapped around each other, bodies gyrating to the music, and in public, to boot? I realized I'd been wrong. Far as *flaunting it* went, homosexuals aint have nothing on the rest of us.

There was a buffet table set up with food and drinks. Dexter got us each a cup of punch. I watched while he took a flask out his pocket and poured some liquor in his. When he offered me some, I shook my head. He downed his punch in one long gulp, then said, "I'm gonna hit the head. You alright?"

I told him I was, and he walked off.

I'd hardly eaten anything at Mrs. Broussard's party, preoccupied as I was. Now I looked at the fried chicken, ribs, candied yams, and collards laid out, and my stomach rumbled. I was reaching toward a stack of plates when I felt somebody bump into me. I whipped around, ready to ask who raised them, and found myself looking Martin Luther King, Jr., smack in the face.

"Beg your pardon, young lady," he said. "I didn't mean to knock into you. I saw those ribs and got a little too excited."

I stared at the man. This was 1960, and he was still mostly a man then, not yet a myth, but he was already in the newspaper all the time, in *Jet* and *Ebony* magazines, and sometimes even on public television. He was a big deal, especially to colored folks, and I was struck dumb for a moment. He looked a lot like he did in photographs, except he wasn't wearing a suit and tie. He was in a white, summery, short-sleeved shirt with seahorses printed on it. He had on what looked like a nice watch. His short hair was slicked back with pomade. He was a little bit shorter than I expected, just like Miss Julia said, but he wasn't small. Still, he wouldn't have stood out much if you didn't already know who he was.

"Oh, it's alright," I said. "I reckon I'll survive."

He'd only glanced at me before, his eyes on the ribs, but now he looked at me straight on. He smiled wide, ran a hand over his slicked-back hair, then held the other hand out to me. "I'm Martin. What can I call you?"

"Doris Steele," I told him.

"Pleasure to meet you, Doris. Have you been enjoying the conference?" he asked me.

I'd barely attended, but I felt ashamed to tell him so. "Yes, sir. Especially the nonviolence workshop. I don't remember the last time I enjoyed something so much." *Lord.* Wasn't anything *enjoyable* about watching folks get cigarette smoke blown in their faces. I sounded about as sharp as a bowl of Jell-O. But he didn't notice. He was still peering at me.

"You have the loveliest dimples," he said.

"Oh. Uh . . . thank you, sir."

"*Sir.* You make me feel like an old man," he said. Then, looking around, he sighed. "Which I suppose I am, more and more every day."

"Oh, no. You aint old," I said, trying to make him feel better. It was true, too. He wasn't but thirty or so. But I reckoned that felt old in a room full of college kids.

His smile came back. "You stay on campus?" he asked me.

I told him I wasn't a college student, and that I was just visiting Atlanta with family.

"How long you here for?" he wanted to know.

"I go home tomorrow."

"You might want to stay a little longer," he said. "There's going to be some very important things happening in Atlanta this week."

"The sit-ins?" I asked, remembering what Dexter had told me. "I aint been trained for that, sir."

"You attended the nonviolence workshop."

"Yes, sir. But I only watched."

He nodded. "Well, there's another workshop on Tuesday, I believe. You could—"

"I *can't,*" I said, and I heard a snap of irritation in my voice.

Reverend King got quiet. After a moment, he asked, "Are you familiar with Joshua, chapter one, verse nine? '*Be strong and courageous. Do not be afraid; do not be discouraged, for the Lord your God will be with you wherever you go.*'"

I knew the verse but it didn't do nothing for me in that moment.

"What we're doing in Atlanta is not just for ourselves but for all Negroes in the Jim Crow South," he said. "Each of us has the power to make change."

But I didn't feel powerful. I felt just the opposite. I was a poor black girl from rural Georgia, pregnant with a baby I didn't want. Everything in my life, from whether or not I could go to school to what water fountain I could drink at to when I became somebody's mama, was for others—Ma and Daddy, white folks, the State of Georgia—to decide. I'd come to Atlanta hoping to be able choose something, but here I was, still pregnant. I couldn't even help myself. How was I supposed to help "all Negroes in the Jim Crow South"?

"Well," Reverend King said, "just because you won't be

here for the sit-ins doesn't mean you can't be part of the movement. There ought to be plenty more opportunities to get involved. Why don't you give me your phone number, and I'll keep you informed of anything that comes—" He stopped suddenly, and grinned, not at me but over my shoulder. "Oh, Corey," he said, "there you are."

When I turned around, there was Coretta Scott King, wearing a tight-lipped smile. "I didn't realize you were looking for me," she said to him. "You seemed deep in conversation over here."

His grin cracked a little along the edges. "I was just talking to . . ."

"Doris."

". . . Doris here, about all the exciting student activity going on in Atlanta right now."

Mrs. King looked at me, and I saw suspicion give way to recognition. "Oh! You're Catie's niece, aren't you?"

I nodded, a little bit surprised she remembered me. We hadn't exchanged but a word or two the other night. "Yes, ma'am," I told her.

"Martin, this is Catie Lucas's niece," she said.

"Catie Lucas?" he asked, sounding distracted, as he started to pile ribs on a plate.

Mrs. King frowned at him, then shook her head. "Never mind." Then, to me, she said, "Are you involved with Snick?"

"Not really, ma'am," I told her.

"Snick is a very important organization," Reverend King said, through a mouthful of pork and barbecue sauce. "Every young person in the Jim Crow South ought to be part of it. That's what I was just telling Doris here."

I felt somebody brush against my shoulder. It was Dexter. "Reverend King," he said, holding out his hand. "Good to see you again, sir." For somebody who "wasn't a follower of King personally," he sure was grinning like a cartoon cat.

Reverend King licked barbecue sauce off his fingers and shook Dexter's hand. "Nice to see you again, Dexter."

"*Dexter,*" Mrs. King repeated to herself, touching her belly. "I've always loved that name."

"How's your uncle?" the reverend asked.

"He's well, sir. I believe he's traveling at the moment."

"Tell him I asked after him."

"I'll do that."

Right then, a man came over. I recognized him as the bodyguard who'd stood outside Mrs. Broussard's house the night Mrs. King was there. That made me think about Erik. And suddenly I remembered what I'd seen earlier, at Erik's house, and I blurted out, "Reverend King, the Klan wants to kill you!"

They all looked at me, surprised by the sudden outburst but not at the fact of the KKK wanting Reverend King dead. "Well, of course they do," he said, and actually laughed.

"I saw something," I told them.

The bodyguard looked at me, all serious now. "Saw what?"

"A meeting," I told them. "Some colored men, some Muslims from up North was meeting with the Klan."

"Where was this?" the bodyguard asked.

"My friend place. I don't know where, exactly. I don't know the streets here."

The bodyguard frowned at me. "So, there was a meeting between the Klan and some Muslims and they, what? Let you sit in? For fun?"

I frowned back at him. He aint have no cause to be rude. "I was in my friend bedroom," I told him. "They aint even know I was there until . . ."

"Until what?"

"Nothing," I said. "Point is, I heard everything."

"What did you hear, Doris?" Mrs. King asked.

"They was talking about working together," I said, "to get land for colored people, separate from whites. Sounded like a bunch of nonsense. But then they started talking about you, Reverend King. The Klan asked the Muslims where you live."

They all looked around at each other now, real concerned, then back at me.

"And what was the Muslims' reply?" Reverend King asked. I could tell by the look on his face that the answer to this question was the one that mattered.

"They say they wasn't gon' tell. They say they wasn't gon' help the Klan do harm to you."

He nodded slowly, and let out a sigh of relief. "Everybody knows the Klan wants me dead. It's good to hear they're not getting help from Negroes to make it happen."

"I find it interesting that the Klan is more worried about you than those Muslims, Reverend King," Dexter said. "Even though everybody knows the Nation of Islam is armed to the teeth. It really tells you something about the power of the nonviolence movement."

They all nodded in agreement. But I didn't think Dexter's point was as sharp as they did. On its face, the Klan feared integration, not separation, so it made sense they were studying Reverend King more. That didn't mean nonviolence was any more effective than armed resistance. And I wasn't sure we ought to rank methods of activism in order of how much they upset the Ku Klux Klan. After everything I'd seen over the last couple of days, from the students at the conference to the men who carried guns to protect them, seemed to me they were all right. It was just a matter of figuring out which one was right for you.

"I'm gonna need the name of your friend," the bodyguard said to me.

"What for?" I asked.

"Just to talk to her," he said. "See what else we can learn about this meeting. What's her name?"

"Erik."

Chile. You would've thought I was loose as an unbuckled belt, the way they all looked at me.

"Erik?" Reverend King asked, sounding scandalized. "That's the name of the friend whose room you were in?"

I couldn't believe it. A married man who'd been trying to get my phone number not three minutes ago, standing there judging *me* about whose bedroom I was in. I'll tell you one thing: I aint ever ceased to be amazed at the *gall* of so-called holy men.

"What's his last name?" the bodyguard asked.

I didn't remember his last name. But it wasn't no way in hell I was telling them that.

"Johnson," Dexter said.

I glanced at him, but he wouldn't look at me. I could tell he was mad about me being with Erik.

"This boy's a Muslim?" the bodyguard asked.

"No," I said. "He wasn't part of the meeting. He aint know nothing 'bout it. They friend, Maurice—"

"*Maurice X?*" Reverend King asked.

"Yes, sir," I said, surprised.

He chuckled, and so did the bodyguard. Even Mrs. King smiled.

"Lil' Maurice always getting involved in some foolishness," Reverend King said. "That's what happens when there are no strong male role models in a boy's life." He shook his head and laughed again. "*Separate land for colored people.* Lord have mercy."

"I'll look into it," the bodyguard said to the reverend. "I'm sure it's a bunch of nothing much, but it's good to keep on top of things."

Reverend King nodded and returned to his food.

"Martin, Julian wants to let you know about security going into next week," the bodyguard told him. "It won't take but a minute."

Reverend King frowned. "Fine. But I'm taking my ribs with me."

The bodyguard pointed at Dexter. "You know where this Erik Johnson lives?"

He nodded.

"Good. I need his address. Come on with me."

The men walked off. As soon as they were gone, Mrs. King's face changed, her eyebrows knitted close together with worry.

"I'm real sorry if I ruined your night, Mrs. King."

"Oh, no," she said, patting me on the arm. "You did the right thing, telling us what you heard." She sighed. "I do fear for Martin's safety. Of course I do. But I also envy him. If he wants to, he can choose to give his very life over to the people."

"That don't sound like nothing to envy," I said. "All due respect, ma'am."

"Oh, but it is," she replied, "when you think about it. Men can give their lives to a cause, or they can keep their lives for themselves. It seems to me that women don't get to choose that way, because our lives already belong to everyone else. We're obligated to our mothers and fathers, our husbands and children, to everyone before ourselves. Our lives are never really ours, to give away or to keep."

That's when I realized this was what I'd been afraid of all along. *This* was why I wanted an abortion. From the first moment, this pregnancy had felt like God forcing me into more obligations. And in that moment, deep in my soul, I rejected it. I rejected it even if it meant rejecting God.

"Doris? Are you alright, hun?" Mrs. King asked me.

I'd felt weak in my knees all of a sudden, and I'd grabbed on to the buffet table to steady myself.

"No, ma'am," I told her. "I'm pregnant and I don't want to be."

And just like that, somebody else knew. And not just any somebody. Coretta Scott King.

"I'm sorry," I said, nodding toward her belly. "I don't want to offend you."

She put her hand on her bump, but she didn't say anything.

"I know it ain't pleasant conversation," I told her. "But what you said, it made me see I don't want to be obligated to nobody before myself no more. I felt guilty 'bout it all this time, too guilty to even see what it was. But why shouldn't I get a say-so for myself?"

Mrs. King had a serious look in her eyes. I couldn't tell what she was thinking. I reckoned I shouldn't have said anything. And, if I *had* to say something, if I just couldn't keep it in, that the pregnant wife of a preacher was the last person I should've said something to. *Lord, Doris.*

But then, Mrs. King took her hand off her belly. She leaned closer to me and whispered, "I know someone. A midwife. A good friend. She can help you."

I stared at her, stunned. "Ma'am?"

"I believe in reproductive freedom for the Negro," she said. She put her hand on her belly again. "Children are a blessing. If you want them. But unwanted children . . . that rarely turns out well for anyone involved, does it?" She reached into her pocketbook and pulled out a piece of paper and a pen, and started writing. "Tell her C.S. gave you the number. And let that be the last time you mention me, hear? If you tell anyone else, I'll have to call you a liar," she said. "And no one will take your word over mine." She held out the paper to me and I took it.

I didn't know what to say. I had no words that seemed like enough. "Thank you."

She reached for my hand and squeezed it. "Send me a letter, will you? When you're settled in back home. I'd love to know you're doing alright. Send it to Ebenezer Baptist Church. They'll pass it on to me."

I nodded. "Yes, ma'am, I'll do that."

"Give Catie my regards," she said, with a kind expression. Then she disappeared into the crowd.

I stood there a minute, staring at the name and number on the little piece of paper, praying for it to be the answer, for this to work out, finally. *Please, Jesus.* I knew it was too late to call now, it would be rude to do so, nobody with any home training would ring somebody up at this hour. But I couldn't stand it. I needed to get it over with, to end this pregnancy and get on with my life, whatever kind of life it was going to be.

I had to walk two blocks to find a pay phone. It was late, but people were enjoying Saturday night, colored Atlantans waiting in line outside swanky-looking places, all dressed to the nines. I tucked myself in a phone booth and plunked in a dime. It rang six times before somebody picked up.

"What you want?" It was a man's voice, sleepy and vexed.

"I'd like to speak to Miss Mitchell, please."

"Somebody in labor?" he asked.

"Naw, sir."

"Somebody dead?"

"Naw."

"What you mean, 'naw'? If it aint nobody in labor, and it aint nobody dead, what you doing calling this time of night? You aint got no home training, girl?"

"Give me the phone, Lester!" a woman's voice called out from the background. A moment later, she came on the line. "Hello?"

"Hello, Miss Mitchell, ma'am. I'm sorry to wake you."

"Who is this?"

"My name Doris," I said. "I'm pregnant. And I . . . don't want to be. Can you help me?"

There was silence for a long moment. Then she said, "Who give you this number?"

"C.S."

Another silence, this one even longer. Then, "You sure you pregnant?"

"Yes, ma'am."

"When was your last menses?"

"Near 'bout the end of August."

"If you sick, I can't do it," she said. "Sick bodies too unpredictable. You healthy? Any problems 'sides this one?"

"Yes, ma'am. I mean, no. No other problems, health-wise. I been having a hard time figuring out what to do with my life, but I don't reckon that's what you mean."

She sort of chuckled at that. "Lord. Come at nine in the morning," she said then. "Bring twenty dollars. If you aint got that, bring what you do got. And I'll take a look at you."

"Take a look?" Maybe it was some kind of code. Maybe she was worried about the law. I doubted the FBI was like to be listening in on a phone call between two colored women in

Georgia at eleven o'clock at night. But I reckon you never know. Better safe than sorry and all that.

"Yes, child. I'll take a look at you to make sure you healthy. Long as you is, I'll bring your menses back."

She gave me her address, and I thanked her.

When I got back to the restaurant, Etta James was floating from the speakers. I stood in the middle of the dance floor, letting her fill me up. I felt my life opening.

Somebody tapped me on the shoulder, and when I turned, there was Dexter.

"Where'd you go?" he asked. "I've been looking for you."

"I had to make a phone call."

"You alright?"

"Sho."

"You want to dance?"

"Yes," I said, and without even thinking about it, I took his hand and pulled him closer.

I'll tell you what: If I had any doubts before about whether he was colored enough, they disappeared while we danced. He moved like kinfolk, from shoulders to hips to feet and back up again.

We danced for what seemed like hours, as the crowd around us got smaller and smaller. Finally, when the only ones left were us and somebody holding a broom, we walked back to Dexter's car, laughing all the way about a whole lot of nothing, the way young folks do in those moments when life feels like it's expanding, stretching, and swelling out before them. "Y'all want the whole world," Mrs. Broussard had said. And right then, I did.

We were still laughing when we got in the car.

"You see how that brother with the broom was looking at us?" Dexter asked. "Looking like, *If y'all don't get y'all asses up out of here!*"

"Poor fella," I said. "He just trying to get home to his family and we in there messing up his life!"

"Shame on us," Dexter said. "We ought to go back and apologize."

I shook my head. "He sho'nuff locked the door already!"

We both fell out, and when we finally pulled ourselves together, Dexter said, "You have to come back to Atlanta real soon. It's better with—"

I kissed him before he could get the rest out. He was shocked for a second, but he caught up quick, slipping his arms around me. Right then and there, I figured out the answer to the one-in-twenty problem: Have more than one man at a time and improve your odds.

We kissed and kissed, the temperature in the car rising all the time. After while, Dexter whispered, "You want to get in the back seat?"

"Sho," I said. "But I don't want to do what you thinking."

He raised his eyebrows. "What you want to do?"

I hesitated. Determined as I was not to let Jesus ruin the moment, I still felt shy about asking. Then I thought about what Miss Julia said about choices, about all the little ones that add up to a life. I wanted a life like hers, a life full of experiences, and I knew just the experience I wanted in that moment.

Problem was, I didn't know what to call it. Miss Julia had said, "Oral sex," but those words didn't make it sound like much fun. She'd also said, "Going down," which sounded more like the beginning of an idea—going down *to the store for cornmeal,* going down *to Macon to visit Aunt Mae*—than a whole plan all by itself. So, I decided to just call it what it was. "I want you to kiss me between my legs," I told him.

A grin spread across his face. "That's *exactly* what I was thinking."

17

The next morning, I woke up from a deep sleep, my first in many days. The paper with the midwife's name and number was on the bedside table where I'd left it. I looked at the clock. It was seven. Nine couldn't come fast enough.

I lay there in my bed for a while, listening to birds singing from nearby trees, and footsteps from the floor above, and thinking about how, in just a couple of weeks, I'd be on a tour bus headed out of Georgia, bound for Memphis and New York City and a different life. It was incredible how, in less than a weekend, so much had changed. I felt curious about the future, interested to see what traveling would be like, but there was also this voice in the back of my mind asking if it was all too good to be true. I thought about my life in Millen, about my family. I knew that when I left on the tour, I'd miss them. I'd miss home. But the idea of missing them also felt good, in the way you sometimes don't eat a cookie until you want it so bad you can't help yourself, and then you enjoy it more. I thought about Lena. I'd miss her as much as anybody else. I fantasized about getting her a job on the tour, too, later, after I'd been there awhile. But I knew she wasn't like me, I knew she already liked the idea of marriage and children and a familiar life. I hoped she'd be happy for me, though. I thought about the last time I'd seen her, how I'd told her about the pregnancy, and I wished it hadn't been so rushed. I suddenly felt the urge to talk to her, to explain myself better, to smooth things over. If I was leaving Millen, I wanted to leave well.

When I got upstairs, neither Mrs. Lucas nor Mrs. Broussard were around. I remembered the night Mrs. Lucas had had, and I reckoned she must be tired. Pearl was in the kitchen making coffee. There was a phone in there, but I didn't want her to hear the call I was about to make. The only other phone I'd seen was in the drawing room, so I went in there and shut the door. I called Lena.

"Hey, Lena," I said when she picked up.

"Doris? You home?"

"Not yet."

"Girl, Miss Babe been worried sick."

"She don't need to worry," I told her. "I'm fine. And I'll be home today."

"And what then?"

"What you mean?"

"I mean, what you gon' tell her when you get back?" Lena asked. "The truth? Or you a liar now, too, on top of killing your own baby?"

I felt a tightness in my chest. It wasn't exactly a shock to me that Lena didn't approve of what I was doing. We hadn't ever discussed abortion, but I knew Lena idealized love, marriage, and children. Still, I hadn't expected this much hostility, and it stunned me.

"Why you even doing this, Doris?" she asked, not waiting for an answer to her first question.

"You know I can't afford no baby, Lena. And I'm too young."

"You seventeen! Plenty girls your age got babies!" The same thing Mrs. Lucas had said. "Besides, what difference do it make? You gon' get married and have kids anyhow, same as everybody else. So, what you even doing all this for?"

"Maybe I *aint* gon' get married and have babies."

She laughed. It wasn't a mean sound. Maybe she just didn't know how else to respond.

"Or maybe I will," I said. "But not now. Not yet."

"'*Not yet*'? You committing a sin bad as this for '*not yet*'? And what about your ma and daddy? What about your brothers? They need you and you done run off."

"I want to try to have a different kinda life," I told her. "I don't know how it's gon' end up. Nobody know that. But I got a right to *try,* aint I?"

"Doris—"

"No," I said. "I don't want to hear nothing else about who need me. I need myself, Lena."

"That don't even make no sense!"

"It make sense to me!" I was almost shouting, and tears were coming to my eyes. Lena was my best friend. I wanted her to see who I was, to understand me. I'd always thought she knew me better than anybody, but these last few days had showed me what it was really like to be seen and now I couldn't settle for something less. I wanted to tell Lena all of that but the words wouldn't come out.

"You never answered my question," she said. "What you gon' tell your ma and daddy when you get back?"

"I don't know what I'm gon' tell them," I said. "And it don't matter no way. What's done is done."

"What you gon' tell Jesus, then?"

I bust out laughing. I couldn't help it. "What I'm gon' tell *Jesus*? To mind his own damn business, that's what!" And I hung up the phone.

A moment later, when Mrs. Lucas walked in, I blurted out, "I found a midwife. She can do my abortion at nine," before she could even say, *Morning, sugar.*

"How? I mean, where did you—"

"Mrs. King gave me her numb—" I stopped. I wasn't supposed to mention Mrs. King. But then I figured since Mrs. Lucas had brought me here, and Mrs. Broussard was paying for it, and they were all friends anyway, everybody was equally guilty in the eyes of the law, or the Lord, so it didn't really matter much if they knew.

Mrs. Lucas looked surprised, and was sure about to ask more questions, but Mrs. Broussard came in and said, "Did you tell her?"

Mrs. Lucas frowned. "I just walked in five seconds ago, Sylvia."

"Right. Sorry."

"Tell me what?" I asked, but somehow I already knew.

Mrs. Lucas stepped toward me. "Pauli got into an argument with Carlton last night. It got . . . out of hand."

"To put it mildly," Mrs. Broussard interjected. "She punched him in the mouth and knocked two of his teeth out."

"He fired her," Mrs. Lucas said.

And suddenly Lena's words seeped in. *It aint gon' make no difference. You gon' get married and have babies anyway. What you even doing this for?*

I thought about last night, about what I'd seen in the hallway. "This *your* fault," I said.

Mrs. Lucas stared at me. I saw something in her eyes I hadn't seen before, at least not directed at me: anger. She opened her mouth to say something but then just stood there.

Behind her, Mrs. Broussard frowned and shook her head. "That's hardly fair, child."

"I *aint* a child!"

"You're sure behaving like one," Mrs. Lucas said.

I felt anger rise in me now. "You the one upset Pauli," I told her. "I saw you."

She squinted her eyes, like a cat getting ready to pounce. I should've shut the hell up. But I kept going.

"You the one trusted Mrs. Broussard when you ought not. You the one dragged me all the way to Atlanta just to get my heart broke!"

"Dragged you? Is that how it went? I seem to remember you begging me for help and refusing to look for it in Millen. I didn't drag you here, Doris. You made a choice to come. And I didn't force you to stay, either. I told you yesterday that I would take you home if you wanted me to."

"But what choice did I have?" I asked, my voice rising now.

"Stay and trust *her*. Or go back to Millen, more pregnant than ever? What kind of choice is that?"

"It's the kind of choice you get sometimes!" she yelled back at me. "If you're lucky enough to have a choice at all! You could've stayed in Millen. You *can* stay in Millen for the rest of your life if you like. You can never *want* anything, and maybe then you'll never be disappointed when something falls apart. But if you make a *choice* to step out into the world, to want things from the world, you better damn well know that disappointment is part of it. And if you are too afraid to face that, then say so, sugar, call it what it is. But don't blame me for that, or Sylvia, when we have done nothing but try to help you."

I wanted to yell some more, I wanted to keep arguing, keep blaming, because I knew the moment I stopped, the moment I accepted that everything she was saying was true, I'd be right back where I started, a poor colored girl who didn't even have the nerve to *dream* of a different life. But I couldn't muster the energy. Leaving Millen was something I'd been curious about. But it hadn't ever been my goal. My goal, if I really had one, was to have space to think about my life and what I might want out of it. But now that the job was gone, I felt despair. I had no other ideas. I felt so tired. I wanted to just curl up in a ball and sob. And then I was crying, tears hot on my cheeks, my lip trembling with grief over a dream I'd only cottoned to a few hours ago and had already lost. "I want to go home," I said.

"What about the midwife?" Mrs. Lucas asked, her voice already softened from moments ago.

I shook my head. "It aint no point."

She came and stood close to me, put her hands on my shoulders.

"I wanted to get rid of it because I didn't want to be obligated to nobody but my own self," I said, between sobs. "But I don't see no path to nothing different. Maybe I'm just too small and afraid, like you said—"

"That's not what I said—"

"But if that's true or not, it washes out to the same thing. I don't have no reason to get rid of it."

Mrs. Lucas let out a long breath. Then she said, "Doris, do you remember when I asked you if you were sure you wanted an abortion?"

"Yes, ma'am."

"Do you remember what you said?"

"I can't afford a baby. And I'm too young."

"That's right, that's what you said. But I wasn't asking *why* you wanted an abortion."

I peered at her, trying to put together what she was getting at.

"Not wanting to be obligated to another person is a good reason for not bringing another person into the world," she said. "But what's also true, Doris, is that you don't *need a reason.* You can have an abortion because you *want one.*"

"Amen to that," Mrs. Broussard said.

"There's plenty things a colored girl can't *have* in this life," said Mrs. Lucas. "But I'll be damned if anybody gets to tell us what we can't *want.* Almost nothing in this world belongs to us, but our desires are ours and we ought not have to explain them to everybody all the damn time. There will always be people demanding to know our reasons, so they can tell us whether they're valid or not. But this is your life. If you *want* an abortion, if you *want* to leave Millen, or stay there, you're allowed to want those things. You don't have to explain why. You hear me?"

"Yes, ma'am."

She got even closer to me and looked me straight in the eyes. "Is an abortion what you want, Doris?"

"Yes, ma'am," I told her. "Yes."

18

The midwife lived in a small house not far from where me and Erik had stood on a porch with loaded guns the evening before. The house had a yellow door and flower boxes outside. Inside, it was small and very neat, with the most spotless white curtains I'd ever seen hanging at the windows. The place smelled like coffee and, at moments, as if drifting in on a breeze, Clorox. They were good smells, familiar and comforting to me as I lay on a table that was covered in a white sheet, a small pillow under my head, staring up at the ceiling of a small room that might have been a dining room, tucked between a living room and kitchen.

Mrs. Mitchell stood over six feet tall, a tree of a woman, with graying hair worn in a long braid down her back and a seriousness in her gaze—when she asked me again if I was sure I was pregnant, and again when my last period had been, and if I'd brought the money—that made me feel she was a person who knew what she was doing, who was in control of the situation, which I especially appreciated when she examined my vagina, and then inserted a speculum.

"Stay still and keep your knees apart, hun."

I did what she said. Soon I felt the dilator being threaded through my cervix, an instrument and a part of my body I hadn't even known the names of an hour ago, before Mrs. Mitchell had told me exactly how this would all go. I breathed slow, trying not to tense up, which wasn't an easy thing. It didn't really hurt but it was uncomfortable. To distract myself, I focused on the small bulge in the side pocket of her dress, the roll of bills I'd paid her with. "I can't believe that's all it costs," Mrs. Broussard had said when I told her. "Herman's fee was four hundred dollars. If this woman hadn't come so highly recommended, I'd be worried."

"Nobody who goes to a granny midwife could pay four hundred dollars, Syl," Mrs. Lucas had said. "But maybe you should pay her double, since she's saving you so much money."

And she did. She really wasn't so bad, Mrs. Broussard.

Mrs. Mitchell took the dilator out and then inserted a curette, a metal rod with a handle on one end and a loop on the other, through my dilated cervix into my uterus.

"Alright now," she said in a serious voice, "this where it starts to hurt. I done this plenty, and I'll be gentle as I can, but I won't lie to you. It aint no picnic. You ready?"

"Yes, ma'am."

She slowly began to scrape the lining of my uterus, and suddenly discomfort became pain. It sure as hell *weren't* no picnic. It was excruciating, a kind of pain I'd never felt in that part of my body. I thought about the births I'd witnessed, the way women screamed and howled, and I wondered if this pain was like that. I couldn't think of another thing that might compare.

I shut my eyes tight and kept breathing, praying to Jesus to just see me through it. And He did. I couldn't tell how long it took. Time seemed to stop at moments, and then start up again slow. But, after while, Mrs. Mitchell removed the curette. And the thing was done.

19

The whole procedure had only taken half an hour—which seemed like a very short time to fix such a very big problem—so it was still early when we returned to Mrs. Broussard's. Mrs. Mitchell had told me that some cramping was to be expected, and to take it easy for a day or two, but that I wouldn't need to stay in bed. Which was lucky because Mrs. Lucas had to be back at work in the morning, and I needed to go home and face my folks. We planned to head to the train station at noon for the twelve-thirty train. Mrs. Broussard told Pearl I was having my time of the month and asked her to fix me some tea with herbs to help with the cramps. I was sitting in the living room, sipping my tea and watching Rocky and Bullwinkle getting into trouble, while Mrs. Lucas sat next to me reading *Annie Allen,* when Dexter came in. I was so shocked to see him walking through the door instead of climbing through the window, I forgot to blush at the thought of what we'd been up to the night before. But soon as he saw me, he started grinning, and my cheeks burned hotter than August.

"Oh, no!" Mrs. Broussard shouted, seeming to appear out

of nowhere. "You better turn your narrow ass around and walk right back on out of here!"

"That's no way to treat family, Auntie Sylvia," Dexter said.

"Boy, *what do you want?*"

"I'm glad you asked. We've had several more people ask to join the sit-ins this week, so I'm helping facilitate a training later today, and another one tomorrow. We could use a little cash for drinks and snacks. It helps with morale."

"You should have plenty for drinks and snacks with the money you got selling our jewelry," Mrs. Broussard said. "You ought to be able to provide Moon Pies and Coca-Colas to every protester in Atlanta and have enough left over for a catered affair."

"Most of that money went to the conference," Dexter said.

Mrs. Broussard just stared at him. He sure did have some nerve.

Mrs. Lucas got up. "I'm happy to donate, let me get my purse."

"Oh, for Christ's sake, Catie!" Mrs. Broussard shouted after her. She cut her eyes at Dexter, then sighed, shook her head, and reached for her own purse.

Maybe Mrs. Broussard was right all along; maybe it didn't make sense for colored folks to fight to eat lunch next to people who hated us. But after looking at it good and hard from all sides over the last couple of days, I reckoned we ought to be able to choose for ourselves, one way or another, even if we chose wrong. And Mrs. Broussard must've known that, too, otherwise she wouldn't have kept giving those kids money.

I remembered what Reverend King had said about each of

us being able to make change for all of us, and how I'd felt powerless to help all colored people when I couldn't even help myself. Now that I'd had the abortion, that feeling of powerlessness had shifted some, and I thought maybe I *could* help. But it still didn't feel like the lunch-counter sit-ins were the way for me to do that.

"You leaving today?" Dexter asked me.

"In a little while."

"I'll get your address from Auntie Sylvia. We can be pen pals if you want."

"She doesn't want," Mrs. Broussard said, handing him a wad of cash.

"I'll have you know, many women find me quite charming," he said to her, and winked at me.

"No, they don't. Now get out," she said, pushing him toward the door. "Before I change my mind about that money."

Mrs. Broussard had arranged a car to take us to the train station, and the same gray-haired man who'd brought us to her house two days before arrived to pick us up. He took Mrs. Lucas's bag, and my pillowcase, down the driveway and waited there for us. Just as we were about to say our goodbyes, Mrs. Lucas realized she'd forgot something in her room and went in to get it. I took the opportunity to ask Mrs. Broussard something I'd been wondering.

"How come you played 'Come Rain or Come Shine' last night? Mrs. Lucas told me about the time Miss Julia sang it for her. You played it for them, aint you?"

She looked a little surprised but she said yes. I asked her why.

"Because Catie needed a *moment,*" she said. "Something to remind her what she's missing, hiding herself away in Millen. I thought dancing with Julia could be it."

Mrs. Lucas reappeared and it was time to go.

"Goodbye, Mrs. Broussard," I said, feeling emotional. "Thank you for what you done. For everything, ma'am. I sho appreciate it." I threw my arms around her.

"Doris, it's been my pleasure," she replied, hugging me back. "If you're ever in Atlanta, come on by."

"Yes, ma'am."

"And you," she said to Mrs. Lucas. "Now that we've patched things up, you'll call me, won't you? And visit?"

"I will."

They hugged.

"You know I love you, Syl. Don't you?" Mrs. Lucas asked.

"Just about," Mrs. Broussard replied, and squeezed her tighter.

20

Three days later, on a Wednesday afternoon, a wave of sit-ins took place all across Atlanta. Like the rest of the protesters, Martin Luther King got arrested that day at Rich's Department Store, in the Magnolia Room, where he and Lonnie King and some others attempted to be served. Unlike some of the others, Reverend King didn't get released that same day. Or the next day. Or the day after that. He got thrown in jail, held on some trumped-up charge about a traffic violation from years before, and sentenced to four months hard labor in state prison.

I wrote to Mrs. King, sending prayers for her family. I reminded her of Proverbs 22:8. "Whoever sows injustice reaps calamity, and the rod they wield in fury will be broken."

I thanked her for her help. I told her that even though I didn't know where my life would take me, I was grateful for the space I had now to imagine a future of my own choosing. I was so thankful to her and all the women who'd helped me.

I never told Ma and Daddy what I'd done. I told them I'd gone to Augusta to help a friend with something she needed to do there, and that I couldn't say what it was because I'd promised. They kept on asking me about it, but I didn't budge. After while, they stopped asking.

One day, I asked Ma and Daddy if they knew anything about the people who'd tried to register to vote in Millen.

"You talkin' bout Hazel?" Ma asked.

"Who Hazel?"

"You know her," Daddy said. "She live right over yonder. Hazel Haley."

"*Mrs. Haley?*" I almost laughed. Crazy enough indeed.

Over the next few months, Ma's condition improved enough that she could do a little more around the house, and I was able to get a part-time job picking tobacco at a farm close by, for extra money. One afternoon, I was walking home from work and I passed Mrs. Haley's house. She was sitting out on her tiny porch, holding a shotgun. It reminded me of myself that day with Erik.

"Afternoon, Mrs. Haley," I called out to her. "Everything alright, ma'am?"

"Doris Steele?" she said, peering at me. "Come on over here, girl."

I'd always avoided Mrs. Haley if I could, and even more so since I'd got back from Atlanta. She was the only person who knew I'd been pregnant, and even though she was crazy and not like to be believed if she told anybody, I didn't want to take the chance. But now she was gesturing me over. I went up on the porch.

"They watching me," she said.

"Who, ma'am?"

"Klan."

I looked around. There wasn't any Klan I could see.

"Naw, they ain't here *now,*" she told me, sounding irritated. "They gone. But they might come back."

"What for?" I asked, unconvinced.

"Teach me a lesson for trying to get on the voter rolls."

"That was last year, ma'am. Why they studying you now?"

"It wasn't no last year. It was yesterday morning."

"You went *back*?"

She nodded, like it was nothing. "Then today, two white men drove right by here, slow, and looked right at me."

I turned and looked out at the road. Everything was quiet. I wished Daddy was home, so I could run over and tell him what Mrs. Haley was telling me. But he was still at work. And Ma had taken the boys to town to get shoes.

When I turned back around, Mrs. Haley was holding out her shotgun. "I got me another one in the house. Take this one and sit with me for a while, would you?"

So, that's what I did. I took the shotgun she offered me, and Mrs. Haley got another one, and we sat on the porch, watching the road. After while, I got up and leaned against the railing.

"You got rid of it, or it got rid of itself?"

When I looked at Mrs. Haley, she was staring at my belly.

I shook my head. "I don't know what you mean, ma'am."

She cackled.

When Daddy got home, I told him what happened, and he told me to go on home, and that he would sit there with Mrs. Haley for a spell. But I told him I didn't want to go, that I was fine right where I was. So, we all sat out there together.

No Klan came that day, or the next, and after a couple days more, we figured that was it. Just a warning. "Don't go back, Hazel," Daddy told her. "You can't be messing with them folks."

She said she wouldn't go back, but I wasn't sure she was telling the truth. I reckoned if she did, I'd sit out there with her again.

Life went on. Nothing was all that different, but everything was different, too. I was different. I thought a lot about that night I'd stood on a porch with the great Julia Avery, talking about love. I played that whole unlikely weekend over in my mind a hundred times. I daydreamed about meeting Miss Julia, and Mrs. King, and even Mrs. Broussard, again someday. And that's not all I daydreamed about. I daydreamed about Dexter's mouth. And Erik's, too. I daydreamed myself in Paris and Memphis and New York City, and back in Atlanta.

When I wasn't daydreaming, I soaked up Millen, put my fingers in its dirt and breathed in its air, and filled a space inside me with it, to keep when I left, which I knew one day I would, even if I still didn't know how, and even if I didn't want to just yet.

Many months after Atlanta, at the beginning of the spring, I got a package in the mail from Miss Julia. In it, there was a brand-new 45 record. The note read: *Hey there, dimples. If you ever write a song you think I could sing, send it to me and I'll take a look. In the meantime, enjoy the song you helped me finish.* I pulled the record out of its sleeve. It was called, "This Broken Heart." I hurried and put it on the record player. Miss Julia's voice filled the room.

When you told me you were leaving
I told myself it wasn't the end
But you forgot me like a song from last summer
And, baby, this broken heart won't ever mend

I listened to the song over and over again. I felt proud. I've written so many songs since then, by myself and with other folks. But that song is special to me, not only for the few words I put in it, but for the way it reminds me of that weekend when everything changed.

Around the same time I received the record, Mrs. Lucas gave notice that she was leaving Burgess Landrum. "I'm moving back to Atlanta," she told me when I came to her classroom to show her the record and the nice note Miss Julia had sent. "Our time there made me realize I've stayed in Millen too long. It was hard to leave after Robert died. There's so much of him here. But there's more of *me* in Atlanta."

That summer, I got a letter from Dexter. He was in Paris, visiting his sister, just like he said he'd be. There was a photograph of them two standing in front of Notre Dame. And there was money. *Use this to buy a plane ticket. Uncle Alonzo hasn't even noticed his watch is missing.*

I laughed so hard I almost peed my pants.

Lena and me never made up, exactly, we just fell back into our usual ways of friendship. She didn't tell Ma and Daddy what I'd done. Weeks and months and years passed, and she didn't tell them. I reckon that's why I felt comfortable enough, after a few years, to tell her some of the details. And, a few years later, a few more. Now, I can't say for sure that Lena was the source of the rumors. She always swore up and down that it wasn't her. But it had to have been somebody who knew a lot about it, and I don't believe it was Mrs. Lucas or Mrs. Broussard. If it wasn't Lena, I got my suspicions who it was, but it aint right to accuse anybody without proof, especially when they're too dead to defend themselves, which everybody who was involved is.

Regardless of who told it, it got told, and told again, and along the way the details went mighty askew. It was winter 1973 when I first heard a version of events that didn't sound anything like what actually happened. It was right after *Roe v. Wade* was passed. Folks was real interested in talking about abortion at that time. A reporter knocked on my door in Atlanta, wanting to ask me about the affair I'd had with Martin Luther King, Jr., and the pregnancy that resulted from it. The way he'd heard it, Mrs. King had been so angry when she found out, she'd demanded I get rid of it. I laughed in the poor man's face. I couldn't help it. I asked where he heard such a ridiculous story, but he said he couldn't reveal his sources. I laughed again. I told the reporter I aint have nothing to report and sent him on his way. Next time I saw Mrs. Lucas, I told her about it.

"My word," she said. "It's only been what? Thirteen years?"

"Mm-hmm. Don't seem like enough time for the truth to evolve into a complete lie, does it?"

Another man came around asking questions in 1980. He was writing a book about Reverend King and said he'd heard "whispers" about a salacious affair with a student activist who got pregnant and got rid of it at the reverend's insistence. Then, in 1992, when the Supreme Court upheld *Roe,* in *Planned Parenthood v. Casey,* another reporter showed up, talking the same nonsense. I wanted to tell her that, yes, I'd had an abortion, and that there were women who helped me, and that those women had given me a gift. That every good thing in my life—every song I'd written, every trip I'd taken, every love I'd chosen—was possible because of that gift. But out of respect for those women, and the secrets I'd promised to keep, all I told her was I never had a relationship with Dr. King. And that I was glad girls weren't being forced to have babies they didn't want anymore.

I used to believe Atlanta changed me. Now I understand that by the time I asked Mrs. Lucas for help, I'd already changed. What changed me was deciding to have an abortion. Knowing, deep in my soul, that what God wanted for me wasn't what I wanted for myself, and that what *I* wanted mattered more, is what lit a new spark in me to question everything else God wanted. Once that happened, life—and God—got a whole lot more interesting.

I still think about that weekend from time to time. I still daydream about it, even now, old as I am. And I never feel silly or small at all. I feel so big.

ACKNOWLEDGMENTS

The character of Doris Steele is based on my grandmother, Doris Wright (née Steele), especially her humor and her way with words. Thank you, Mom-Mom, for inspiring me, both in this life and from the next.

Thank you to Meredith Coleman-Tobias, Melissa Colbert, and especially CarmenLeah Ascencio, for all the ways y'all show up for me in queer family and community.

Thank you to my favorite living Southerner, Dr. Chassidy Bozeman, for loving me and making me happy while I was writing this book.

Thank you to my editor and friend, Caitlin McKenna; and to my literary agent, Alexa Stark.

And to my children, Story and Rio, thank you for making me laugh every single day. If I could choose any life, I'd always choose the one where I get to be your mama.

ABOUT THE AUTHOR

Mia McKenzie is the two-time Lambda Award–winning author of *The Summer We Got Free* and *Skye Falling,* and the creator of Black Girl Dangerous Media, an independent media and education project that centers queer Black women and girls. She lives with her two children near Amherst, Massachusetts.

mia-mckenzie.com
X: @miamckenzie

ABOUT THE TYPE

This book was set in Baskerville, a typeface designed by John Baskerville (1706–75), an amateur printer and typefounder, and cut for him by John Handy in 1750. The type became popular again when the Lanston Monotype Corporation of London revived the classic roman face in 1923. The Mergenthaler Linotype Company in England and the United States cut a version of Baskerville in 1931, making it one of the most widely used typefaces today.